WITHDRAWN

A Day No Pigs Would Die

Robert Newton Peck

A Day No Pigs Would Die

Alfred·A·Knopf New York
1981

THIS IS A BORZOI BOOK
PUBLISHED BY ALFRED A. KNOPF, INC.

Copyright © 1972 by Robert Newton Peck

Library of Congress Cataloging in Publication Data

Peck, Robert Newton. A day no pigs would die.
I.   Title.
PZ4.P3675Day   [PS3566.E254]   813'.5'4   72–259
ISBN 0–394–48235–2

Part of Chapter Fourteen originally appeared in *The Atlantic Monthly*.

Manufactured in the United States of America
PUBLISHED, JANUARY 10, 1972
REPRINTED SEVEN TIMES
NINTH PRINTING, JANUARY 1981

To my father, Haven Peck . . .
a quiet and gentle man
whose work was killing pigs.

A farmer's heart is rabbit soft,
And farmer eyes are blue.
But farmers' eyes are eagle fierce
And look a man right through.

A Day No Pigs Would Die

Chapter

I

I should of been in school that April day.

But instead I was up on the ridge near the old spar mine above our farm, whipping the gray trunk of a rock maple with a dead stick, and hating Edward Thatcher. During recess, he'd pointed at my clothes and made sport of them. Instead of tying into him, I'd turned tail and run off. And when Miss Malcolm rang the bell to call us back inside, I was halfway home.

Picking up a stone, I threw it into some bracken ferns, hard as I could. Someday that was how hard I was going to light into Edward Thatcher, and make him bleed like a stuck pig. I'd kick him from one end of Vermont to the other, and sorry him good. I'd teach him not to make fun of Shaker ways. He'd never show his face in the town of Learning, ever again. No, sir.

A painful noise made me whip my head around and jump at the same time. When I saw her, I knew she was in bad trouble.

It was the big Holstein cow, one of many, that belonged to our near neighbor, Mr. Tanner. This one he called "Apron" because she was mostly black, except for the white along her belly which went up her front and around her neck like a big clean apron. She was his biggest cow, Mr. Tanner told Papa, and his best milker. And he was fixing up to take her to Rutland Fair, come summer.

As I ran toward her, she made her dreadful noise again. I got close up and saw why. Her big body was pumping up and down, trying to have her calf. She'd fell down and there was blood on her foreleg, and her mouth was all thick and foamy with yellow-green spit. I tried to reach my hand out and pat her head; but she was wild-eyed mean, and making this breezy noise almost every breath.

Turning away from me, she showed me her swollen rump. Her tail was up and arched high, whipping through the air with every heave of her back. Sticking out of her was the head and one hoof of her calf. His head was so covered with blood and birthsop that I had no way telling he was alive or dead. Until I heard him bawl.

Apron went crashing through the puckerbush, me right behind. I'd never caught up. But because she had to stop and strain, I got to the calf's head and got a purchase on him.

He was so covered with slime, and Apron was so wandering, there was no holding to it. Besides, being just twelve years old, I weighed a bit over a hundred pounds. Apron was comfortable over a thousand, and it wasn't much of a tug for her. As I went down, losing my grip on the calf's neck, her hoof caught my shinbone and it really smarted. The only thing that made me get up and give the whole idea another go was when he bawled again.

I'd just wound up running away from Edward Thatcher and running away from the schoolhouse. I was feathered if I was going to run away from one darn more thing.

I needed a rope. But there wasn't any, so I had to make one. It didn't have to be long, just strong.

Chasing old Apron through the next patch of prickers sure took some fun out of the whole business. I made my mistake of trying to take my trousers off as I ran. No good. So I sat down in the prickers, yanked 'em off over my boots, and caught up to Apron. After a few bad tries, I got one pantleg around her calf's head and knotted it snug.

"Calf," I said to him, "you stay up your ma's hindside and you're about to choke. So you might as well choke getting yourself born."

Whatever old Apron decided that I was doing to

her back yonder, she didn't take kindly to it. So she started off again with me in the rear, hanging on to wait Christmas, and my own bare butt and privates catching a thorn with every step. And that calf never coming one inch closer to coming out. But when Apron stopped to heave again I got the other pantleg around a dogwood tree that was about thick as a fencepost.

Now only three things could happen: My trousers would rip. Apron would just uproot the tree. The calf would slide out.

But nothing happened. Apron just stood shaking and heaving and straining and never moved forward a step. I got the other pantleg knotted about the dogwood; and like Apron, I didn't know what to do next.

Her calf bawled once more, making a weaker noise than before. But all old Apron did was heave in that one place.

"You old bitch," I yelled at her, grabbing a dead blackberry cane that was as long as a bullwhip and big around as a broom handle, "you move that big black smelly ass, you hear?"

I never hit anybody, boy or beast, as I hit that cow. I beat her so hard I was crying. Where I held the big cane, the thorns were chewing up my hands real bad. But it only got me madder.

I kicked her. And stoned her. I kicked her again one last time, so hard in the udder that I thought I heard her grunt. Both her hind quarters sort of hunkered down in the brush. Then she started forward, my trousers went tight, I heard a rip and a calf bawl. And a big hunk of hot stinking stuff went all over me. Some of it was calf, some of it wasn't.

As I went down under the force and weight of it, I figured something either got dead or got born.

All I knew was that I was snarled up in a passel of wet stuff, and there was a strong cord holding me against something that was very hot and kicked a lot. I brushed some of the slop away from my eyes and looked up. And there was Apron, her big black head and her big black mouth licking first me and then her calf.

But she was far from whole. Her mouth was open and she was gasping for air. She stumbled once. I thought for sure I was going to wind up being under a very big cow. The noise in her throat came at me again, and her tongue lashed to and fro like the tail of a clock. It looked to me as if there was something in her mouth. She would start to breathe and then, like a cork in a bottle, some darn thing in there would cut it off.

Her big body swayed like she was dizzy or sick. As the front of her fell to her knees, her head hit my chest as I lay on the ground, her nose almost touching my chin. She had stopped breathing!

Her jaw was locked open so I put my hand into her mouth, but felt only her swollen tongue. I stretched my fingers up into her throat—and there it was! A hard ball, about apple-size. It was stuck in her windpipe, or her gullet. I didn't know which and didn't care. So I shut my eyes, grabbed it, and yanked.

Somebody told me once that a cow won't bite. That somebody is as wrong as sin on Sunday. I thought my arm had got sawed off part way between elbow and shoulder. She bit and bit and never let go. She got to her feet and kept on biting. That devil cow ran down off that ridge with my arm in her mouth, and dragging me half-naked with her. What she didn't do to me with her teeth, she did with her front hoofs.

It should have been broad daylight, but it was night. Black night. As black and as bloody and as bad as getting hurt again and again could ever be.

It just went on and on. It didn't quit.

Chapter

2

"Haven Peck."

Somebody was yelling out Papa's name, but I couldn't see anything. And it was real strange, because my eyes were open. They sort of stinged. So I blinked, but the fog was still there.

There was a wool blanket around me. I could feel the wool rub against the raw place on my arm, but the hurt of it seemed to keep me awake. And keep me alive.

There were more voices now. I heard Papa answer, and the man who was carrying me asked him, "Is this your boy? There's so much blood and dirt and Satan on him, I can't tell for sure. Besides, he's near naked."

"Yes," said Papa. "That's our Robert."

And then I heard Mama's voice, soft and sweet like music; and I could feel her hands on my head and my hair. Aunt Carrie was there, too. She was Mama's oldest sister, who lived with us.

Strong hands were touching my legs now, and then my ribs. I tried to say something about not being in school. Somebody had some warm water and washed my face with it. The water had lilac in it, and smelled right restful.

"We're beholding to you, Benjamin Tanner," said Papa, "for fetching him home. Whatever he done, I'll make it right."

"Better look to his arm. It got tore up worse than proper. May be broke."

"Haven," I heard Mama say, "the boy's holding something in his hand. Can't make it out."

I felt them taking something from my right hand. I didn't want to render it up, but they took it.

"I never see the like of it," Mama said. "Like it's near to be alive."

I could hear Mr. Tanner's rough voice over the others. "I know what that is. It's a goiter."

"Goiter?"

"Where'd he get it?"

"It's an evil thing. But for now let's tend his arm. Mr. Tanner, we may got to cut away part of your blanket."

"Ain't mine. Belongs to my horse. So cut all you're a mind to."

I felt Papa pulling the blanket down off my right shoulder, until it got caught in the clotted blood. I heard his jackknife click open, and cut away part of the wool.

"I tied my bandana on his arm," said Mr. Tanner, "so he wouldn't bleed dry." When Papa loosened it up, Mr. Tanner said, "He'll bleed again with it loose, Haven."

"He will," said Papa, "and that'll be a good thing for his arm. Let it open up and holler out all the dirt. Only way to treat a wound is to bleed it, 'til it's clean as a cat's mouth."

"True."

"Lucy," Papa spoke soft to Mama, "better get a needle threaded. He'll want sewing."

He picked me up in his arms, carried me into the house and to the kitchen. He laid me flat on the long lammis table, face up. Mama put something soft under my head, and Aunt Carrie kept washing me off with the lilac water while Papa cut off my shirt and took off my boots.

"The poor lamb," said Mama.

Somebody put a hand on my forehead to see if I was cool. It was followed by a cold wet cloth, and it felt real good. Funny, but it was the only thing on my entire body that I could feel. Then I felt the first of Mama's stitches going into the meat of my arm.

I wanted to yell out, but didn't have the will for it. Instead I just lay there on my back on that old kitchen table and let Mama sew me back together. It hurt. My eyes filled up with crying and the water ran in rivers to my ears, but I never let out a whimper.

When I had took all the sewing to be took (and by this time I must of been more thread than boy) Papa burdened me upstairs to my room. I could smell Mama, crisp and starched, plumping my pillow, and the cool muslin pillowcase touched both my ears as the back of my head sank into all those feathers.

"Tell Mr. Tanner," I said.

Mama rushed to where my head was, and Papa and Aunt Carrie were at bed foot.

"Tell Mr. Tanner," I said again, "that were he to look up on the ridge, he'll find a calf. I helped get it born. Afterward, old Apron was still choking so I had to rip the ball out of her throat. And I didn't mean to skip school."

"I'll be," said Papa.

"Where are your trousers, Rob?" said Aunt Carrie, who took quite a stock in appearances.

"Up on the ridge. When I tied 'em round a tree they got busted some. I'm sorry, Mama. You'll just have to cut me out another pair."

Mama put her face right down close to mine, and I could smell her goodness.

"I'm preferenced to mend busted pants than a busted boy."

"I . . . I can't feel nothing in my right hand."

"That's 'cause it's resting," said Mama. "It wants to get well, and so do you. So right about now your Pa and Carrie and I are going to tiptoe out of here and let you get some rest. You earned it."

They left. And I closed my eyes and went right off. Later I woke up when Mama brought me a dish of hot succotash and a warm glass of milking, fresh from the evening pail. The bubbles were still on it.

"That's real good," I said.

At bedtime, Papa came upstairs with his big shoes kicking one of the risers, and brought me one of the last of the winter apples from the cellar. He pulled up a chair close to my bed and looked at me for a long time while I ate the apple with my left hand.

"You mending?"

"Yes, Papa."

"I ought to lick you proper for leaving the school-house."

"Yes, Papa. You ought."

"Someday you want to walk into the bank in Learning and write down your name, don't you?"

"Yes, sir."

"I don't cotton to raise a fool."

"No, Papa."

I tried to move my right arm, but it made me wince up. I couldn't help but make a noise about it.

"She bit you up fair, that cow. Clear to bone."

"Sure did. I always thought cows don't bite."

"Anything'll bite, be it provoked."

"I guess I provoked old Apron. Boy, she sure did some provoking on me."

"You put a hand in her mouth?"

"Yes."

"You rip out that . . . goiter?"

"Yes, sir."

"Was that 'fore or after the calfing?"

"I disremember. All I recall is that Apron was choking something fearful with a piece of stuff in her throat that she wanted me to fetch out."

"So you tore out that goiter."

"Yes, sir. Her calf was hung up, too. So I tore him out. Tore my pants and tore myself. Between me and the calf and Apron, we tore up a good part of Vermont as well as each other."

"How do you feel?"

"Like if I die, at least I'll stop hurting."

"Best you don't complain, a boy who skips school and don't get no stick put on him."

"No, sir. I won't complain. Except when I move

it sharp and sudden, my arm is real numb. It's the rest of me that's in misery."

"Where?"

"My backside and my privates. I'm stuck so full of prickers, it makes me smart just to think on it. Every damn—"

"What'd I hear?"

"Every darn pricker in Vermont must be in me, working their way through, and coming out the yonder side. It's enough to sell your soul."

"Well, if your soul looks as poorly as your carcass, I don't guess it'll bring much."

"I don't guess it will."

Papa fished around in his pocket.

"Here's two beads of spruce gum. One's for me. But I don't mention you'd want one."

"Yes, I sure would. Please."

"Here, then. Might help you forget where those prickers are nested."

"It's helping already. Thanks, Papa."

The spruce gum was hard and grainy at first. Then the heat of your mouth begins to melt it down so that it's worth the chewing. The bit that Papa gave me was rich and full of sappy juices. Except that every so often you have to spat out a flick of the bark.

"I saw sumac today, boy."

"Is it ripe yet?"

Out of his pocket, Papa pulled a twig of sumac that was finger-thick and four-inch long.

"How's that look?"

"Papa, that looks real good. Got your knife?"

Papa cracked out his knife, ringed the bark, and set a good notch at one end. All there was left to do now was to bucket soak it overnight, just enough to slip the bark sleeve. And boil it to kill the poison.

"That'll be some whistle, Robert."

"Sure will."

"A boy with a whistle as fine as this won't have no earthy reason to skip school. You of a mind to agree?"

"I agree, Papa."

He stood up, big and tall with his head not quite bumping the roof of my bedroom.

"Don't be going to sleep with spruce gum in your mouth."

"I won't, Papa."

He bent down and pulled the crazy quilt up around my throat. I could tell by the smell of his hand that he'd killed pigs today. There was a strong smell to it, like stale death. That smell was almost always on him, morning and night. Until Saturday, when he'd strip down to the white and stand in the kitchen washtub, up to his shins in hot soapy water, and wash himself clean of the pigs and the killing.

He smelled the best on Sunday morning, when I sat next to him at Shaker Meeting. He smelled just like the big brown bar of soap that he used, and sometimes there was some store-bought pomade on his hair. But when you kill pigs for a living, you can't always smell like Sunday morning.

You just smell like hard work.

Chapter

3

I was abed for almost a week.

My first day up was Saturday. I planned it that way so I'd have me two days out of bed and out of doors, without a mind for schooling.

"Good," said Papa when he saw me hobble down to breakfast in the kitchen. "I can use a hand, and you look ready as rain."

I limped a bit more than need be, but it didn't do a lick of good. An hour later, we were resetting a post in the fence that set Mr. Tanner's land apart from ours.

"Fences sure are funny, aren't they, Papa?"

"How so?"

"Well, you be friends with Mr. Tanner. Neighbors and all. But we keep this fence up like it was war. I guess that humans are the only things on earth that take everything they own and fence it off."

"Not true," Papa said.

"Animals don't put up fences."

"Yes, they do. In the spring, a female robin won't fly to a male until he owns a piece of the woods. He's got to fence it off."

"I didn't know that."

"Lots of times when you hear that old robin sing, what he's singing about is . . . keep off my tree. That whistle you hear is his fence."

"Gee."

"Ever see a fox?"

"Sure. Lots of times."

"I mean really watch him. He walks around his land every day and wets on a tree here and on a rock there. That's his fence. I can't tell of any more than that, but my guess would be that all living things put up a fence, one way or another. Like a tree do with its roots."

"Then it isn't like war."

"It's a peaceable war. If I know Benjamin Franklin Tanner, he'd fret more than me if his cows found my corn. He'd feel worse than if it was the other way round."

"He's a good neighbor, Papa."

"And he wants a fence to divide his and mine, same as I do. He knows this. A fence sets men together, not apart."

"I never looked at it that way."

"Time you did."

As we were talking, I looked up from my work and Papa from his. What we saw was the oddest parade in the county, coming down the ridge and across the meadow. It was Ben Tanner and his cow, Apron. She was looking clean as clergy. Kicking along under her belly and trying to get hold of a teat was not one calf, but two! Alike as two peas. And Mr. Tanner was carrying something.

"Morning, Haven."

"A day to you, Benjamin."

"Morning, young Rob."

"Morning, Mr. Tanner."

I wasn't really looking at our neighbor as I spoke. What caught my eye was the finest pair of bull calves you could ever try to see. They were blacker than Apron, but with a patch of clean white up the front, like a chin napkin.

"Bob and Bib," said Mr. Tanner. "And the Bob of it is after you, Robert."

"Well now," said Papa.

"A matched pair, they be. Always wanted a yoke of matched Holstein oxen to take to Rutland. Now, thanks to your stout son, Haven, I got me the pair. Finest oxen in the county, they be. And come Fair time a year, they'll do Learning proud."

"Apron had *two?*" It was all I could say.

"Two, and that's all. But they right there, balls or no balls, make a pretty pair of bull calves. And Robert, I thank you again. Here's a pig for your trouble."

From under his coat, Mr. Tanner fetched out a small white ball of piglet. She had a pink nose and pink ears, and there was even a wisp or two of pink in the fork of her toes.

"You mean—this pig is going to be *mine?*"

"Yours, my boy. Little enough for what you did."

"Gosh'em Moses. Thanks, Mr. Tanner."

Mr. Tanner handed me the pig and I took it. She kicked and squealed a bit, but once I held her close up to my chest with both arms, she settled down and licked my face. Her spit was a sad smell, but I didn't care. She was *mine.*

"We thank you, Brother Tanner," said Papa. "But it's not the Shaker Way to take frills for being neighborly. All that Robert done was what any farmer would do for another. It don't add up to payment or due."

I felt sick. Real sick. Papa wasn't going to let me have her.

"Haven, when is the boy born?"

"February," I said, before Papa could answer.

"Plum forgot," said Mr. Tanner. "In that case, I

owe you a sorry to be so late remembering. She's
your pig, Robert. And if I catch her on my land
again, she'll be bacon."

Papa shook his head. "It's not right."

"Haven Peck," said Mr. Tanner, "what I really
come here for is to ask you to help me yoke these
two demons come fall. Will you?"

"Yes," said Papa.

"Good, good. That being the case, and not wanting the cloud of debt hanging over me, favor me by
taking payment for your help as of now in the form
of one newborn pig, just weaned, in pink of prime."

"Done," said Papa.

"Done," I said.

At that, the pig and I both gave a squeal. She was
mine, mine, mine, mine, *mine!*

Looking at her again, I could now see how beautiful she was. My pig. She was prettier than Apron, or
either one of her calves. She was prettier than Solomon, our ox. Prettier than Daisy, our milk cow.
Prettier than any dog or cat or chicken or fish in the
whole township of Learning, Vermont. She was
clean white all over, with just enough pink to be
sweet as candy.

"Pinky," I said.

"Fine name," said Mr. Tanner. "And every whit
as good as Bob and Bib."

"Benjamin," said Papa, "we're beholding."

"Thank you, sir," I said. Papa's sharp nudge in my ribs with the handle of his mattock helped my being so prompt and grateful.

"Welcome, boy. And if I ever need help again, with old Apron here in calf, there's only one man I'd call to help her through."

"Who?" I said, knowing the answer.

"You," he said, pinching my stomach that I laughed so hard I almost dropped Pinky.

Watching our neighbor walk away, taking his cow and twin calves with him, I held Pinky close in my arms. She was the first thing I had ever really wanted, and owned. At least, the first thing of value. The only other thing I'd wanted was a bicycle, but I knew we couldn't afford it, so there was no sense in asking. Besides, both Mama and Papa would have looked at a bicycle as a work of the Devil. A frill. And in a Shaker household, there wasn't anything as evil as a frill. Seemed to me the world was full of them. But anything that Mama wanted and didn't have the money to buy (or the goods to trade for) was a frill to her.

Well, nobody could call Pinky a frill. Anybody who had half an eye could see she was a pig. And what a brood sow she'd make. I counted the teat buds on her belly. Twelve. In a year or so, she'd be lying in her crib with a dozen pigs sucking away for glory be.

"You'll have to tend care of her," Papa said.

"I will."

"Care taking of a pig can keep a body as nervous as a longtail cat in a room full of rocking chairs. She'll need a pen, and some straw."

"A pen?"

" 'Course a pen. Where'd you think she'll sleep? Under your pillow?"

"No. But I thought she could bed up with Solomon and Daisy."

"Can't keep swine and kine under the same roof. Says so in the Book of Shaker. That means that you, Robert, are going to make her a place."

"Well, it won't have to be very big."

"Not today, it won't. But do you idea how big she'll get? Before you know it, she'll weigh twenty stone."

"Twenty stone. That's a lot!"

"Durn right. She'll go most three hundred. So best you put that pig down to earth, set that fencepost, and pen her up for night. Away from Daisy."

"Why that?"

"Close pork will curdle milk, boy. That's plain common."

"I wonder why that is."

"It's just a law."

"Shaker Law?"

"Yes, but deeper than that. It goes back when Daisy and Pinky were wild. Daisy knows that Pinky and her kind have teeth. Tusk. And pigs are meat eaters, cows ain't. The reason Brother Tanner give you that pig is maybe its mother ate all the rest of the litter. A sow will do that. Daisy won't. Apron won't. It's like Shaker Law. It all goes way back."

"Way back to what?"

"Back to reason. Something that modern townfolk don't care a lick for. They don't understand it, so they think it to be tomfool."

"Back to reason."

"That's right as rain. It's earthy reason. Solomon's got it at sundown, and that's the only time of day that big ox is ornery. Because once, long long ago, the wolves came at sundown. Even though Solomon never seen a wolf, he knows. He knows that workaday is over, and that he wants shelter. He wants a wall at his side so he can blanket one flank and look the other."

"And that's why Daisy won't want Pinky near on?"

"That's why. Because pigs are wild things. Were you to turn Pinky loose, she'd live in the hills. And she'd be wild. She'd even tusk, and they'd be long and mean and sharp. And old Daisy knows it. And frets on it. She says it's enough to curdle a girl's milk."

"Papa?"

"Huh."

"If Daisy run off, would she be a wild cow?"

"Not old Daisy. If we left her, she'd head for another farm and another herd. She might make for Tanner's place. You know what she'd do. She'd wait for night and then head for a lighted house. The orange window of home and hearth."

"You sure?"

"Well, you remember when we went camping out all night, all the way up on top of Lead Hill?"

"I remember. That was fun."

"You recall our bonfire? How big it was?"

"Sure do."

"What animal come to us in the night, just to share our flame, and you thought it was a bear?"

"A *cow*."

"You'd had a gun that night, you'd a shot some farmer's sweet old cow right between the tits."

"Papa, you recall what we did when that old cow stayed next to us all night?"

"Come firstlight, we milked a bit of her. So you could have a cup of fresh warm milk for breakfast. And I could have a spoonful for my coffee."

"Was that stealing, Papa?"

"Not hardly. Were it my cow, I'd share with others. And we didn't take but a glass. It weren't as though we stripped her dry."

"Do you think the Lord will forgive us?"

"I think so. Somehow, the Good Lord don't want to see no man start a cold morning with just black coffee."

Chapter

4

Pinky sure got to be my pig in a heck of a hurry.

Papa and I had to finish our job that we started that Saturday morning, which was to reset the East fence. So after our neighbor, Mr. Tanner, took his leave, we worked for a piece.

All the time I was working, Pinky was smelling around near my heels, keeping her little pink nose to the ground as all pigs do. It was hard to get any work done, the way Pinky was rubbing against my boots. Just like a cat. And when we quit at church-bell for the noon meal, she followed us all the way across the East meadow to the house. I was going to bring her into the kitchen, but Mama put her foot down on that idea.

Before we ate, I mixed a bowl of milk and meal for Pinky to eat. It was real soppy and mostly milk. I didn't think she was going to take it at first. But after I dipped my finger in it and let her suck away on that, she went for the bowl. I made sure that the bowl I used was the cracked one, or I'd a got skinned.

Both Mama and Aunt Carrie confessed that Pinky was just about the prettiest pig they ever saw.

"Pinky's a fitting name," said Mama.

"Never heard of naming a pig," Aunt Carrie said.

"But Solomon has a name," I said, "and so do Daisy."

"Let's eat," Papa said, "before we have to name every weed on the place."

After meal, Papa headed out toward the barn with Pinky and me trailing along behind. He walked round the barn a yoke of times, and come to a final rest on the South side of it. He put his foot on a stump, elbow to his knee, and looked real hard at our old corn cratch.

"What you got a mind to, Papa?"

"Rob, that there crib would make a good house for your pig. 'Cept it's a mite too close to the cow barn."

"Close? It's touching it, butt on."

"Lucky, it's on skids. We can drag her."

"Papa, we can't drag that. We only got one ox."

"Solomon can do it, if we help."

"We're going to yoke us up next to Solomon?"

"No, Solomon don't need muscle help. What we're

— 29 —

going to give him, boy, is some extra thinking. We're going to let Solomon use a capstan—just a great big crank."

"Like you use at Aunt Matty's to wind up the well water?"

"Like that. Go get Solomon, and mind his hoofs."

I was bringing Solomon over to the barn, leading him with just my hand on his horn, and taking two steps to his one. Then I went round to the tackroom to get his yoke and stays. The yoke was solid hickory and it weighed near as much as me. I had to lug it round back in two trips, going back the second time for the oxbow and cotter. Papa showed up with two long poles, a chain, and a digger.

With the posthole digger (which looked to me like a big corkscrew) he twisted a hole into the ground, down the meadow a ways from the corn cratch. Using a pebble on a horsehair string, he dropped it deep in the hole and let it hung to see if the hole was plumb to the earth. Then deep into the hole he sunk one of the stout poles. So stout it was nigh to be a log. Papa said the post was about "three hands around." This was the capstan's axle.

Next came the tongue and this log would be the crank handle. Papa fit the handle pole into a hole (just up from ground flush) in the axle.

"That do it, Papa?"

"That do her. Solomon ready?"

"I need help, Papa. I can't put the yoke up on his shoulders by myself. How much it weigh?"

"Oh, maybe six stone."

"That's as much as I weigh."

"Almost."

Solomon was yoked and coupled to the capstan crank. We were ready.

"So," said Papa, "you don't guess one ox can pull that there crib?"

"No," I said. "It's too blundersome. Not even Mr. Tanner's bay Belgian team could move it, if you want my study of it."

Papa clucked to Solomon and he leaned into yoke. The crank began to turn. Around and around Solomon walked in a circle, and the chain drawed up real snug. When it was tight, it snapped up off the ground, but old Solomon never stopped walking. After just once around, Papa made a trench for the chain so Solomon wouldn't have to step over it with every circle. The big ox needed no ·prodding. He walked the circle on his own, and the crib inched toward the axle post.

"Look, Papa. Solomon does it alone."

"He does for sure. Solomon told me he don't want no pig having sleeping quarters near his. He says he abides in Shaker Law."

"Papa, do you believe all the Shaker Law?"

"Most. I'm glad it's all writ down in the Book of Shaker."

"How do you know it's all writ down, Papa? You can't read."

Papa looked at me before he spoke.

"No, I cannot read. But our Law has been read to me. And because I could not read, I knew to listen with a full heart. It might be the last and only time I'd learn its meaning."

"I don't cotton to all those Shaker Laws. Especially one."

"Which one?"

"The one that says we can't go to the baseball game on Sunday. Jacob Henry and his father always go. Why can't we?"

"Rob, the Book of Shaker forbids frills on any day. And that goes double on Sunday."

"But we wouldn't be *playing* baseball. Just watching. And I want to see the Greemobys play."

"What's a Greemoby?"

"It's short for Green Mountain Boy. It got something to do with somebody called Ethan Allen. I guess he was once the captain. Or the shortstop."

"I don't understand one breath of it," said Papa.

"I do. Our school library has this book on the history of baseball. There was a lot in it about Abner Doubleday, but it sure was skimpy on Ethan Allen."

"I wouldn't know one of them baseballers from the other."

"Well," I said, "if you put any stock in this book I read, it sure leads a body to believe that Ethan Allen wasn't anyone at all. And that Abner Doubleday did everything there was to be did. But that's where I went sour on the history test that Miss Malcolm give us."

"You told your Ma and me you got the highest in that test. Were you falsing a witness, Rob?"

"No, sir. I did get the highest mark. I got a ninety-nine. There was a hundred questions and I only missed one. It was something about which Vermonter *played* a key part in our history. The answer was somebody else. But since I read that book, I just put down the name of Abner Doubleday."

" 'Stead of Ethan Allen."

"That's right, Pa. How'd you know?"

"Just a guess."

"Well, I took a guess too. And it sure was wrong. When Miss Malcolm handed the papers back, she was laughing."

"At what?"

"At me and Abner Doubleday."

"Oh."

Solomon kept walking his circle, pulling the old corn cratch closer to the capstan post with every turn. The post was now fat with the twines of black chain. That old ox sure could pull aplenty. He wound up that big chain just like you'd wind a kite string around a spool.

"Papa, it sure is mirthful that somebody who knows history like Miss Malcolm knows it has never heard of a great man like Abner Doubleday. She even asked me who he was."

"I s'pose you thought it be your calling to tell her."

"Sure did. But one thing certain—of the two men, Miss Malcolm tends to favor Ethan Allen. Which one do you like, Papa?"

"Can't say honest that I take to either one."

"Miss Malcolm sure does. She says that seeing we live in a free country like Vermont, we all better be proud as pie over Ethan Allen and his Green Mountain Boys. That's his baseball team."

"The pursuit of history sure has a foggy sound to it," said Papa, watching the chain thicken round the capstan post. "Makes no sense to me."

"Well, it all makes clear to me. Except the part about Ethan and his baseball team. They won at Ticonderoga."

"I know of that."

"So does Miss Malcolm. I was getting poked in the back by Will Stoddard, so I didn't rightly get the straight of it. But I do recall this much. In the middle of the night, old Ethan took his team crosslake to Ticonderoga, and they stayed the night in a fort."

"Thanks be praised all the history I need's in our Family Bible tucked away under the bed in the Bible Box. And in the Book of Shaker."

"I guess it's history that calls us to move this here cratch for Pinky, eh Papa?"

"It's reason."

"A long time ago, somebody broke the Shaker Law and put up a cow and a pig together, and they had one walloping fight."

"Maybe so," said Papa.

"I wonder who won."

"A boar's got a blessed mean mouth."

"I question who'd win if Ethan Allen met up with Abner Doubleday. I can conjur who Miss Malcolm would root for."

"Ethan Allen?"

"That's for certain. She says that 'cuz we're all Vermonters, we have to be proud of our yesterday just like today."

"What's that mean?"

"I think it means to be proud to live in Vermont, and proud of Ethan Allen. As well as that other fellow she talks on, the one who lives in a white house."

"Lots of folks in Learning live in a white house."

"I think Miss Malcolm means Calvin Coolidge. We have to pride him too."

"Say we do. He's our President."

"Miss Malcolm said she voted for Calvin Coolidge, which is why he's a President. She says that every working soul in Vermont voted for him."

"Not all."

"Did you vote for Calvin Coolidge, Papa?"

"No."

"Aren't you a Republican? Just about everybody is in the whole town of Learning."

"No, I'm not a Republican. And I'm not no Democrat. I'm not nothing."

"Why not?"

"Because I'm not allowed to vote."

"Me either. You have to be twenty-one to vote. I'm only twelve."

"Reckon I'm soon looking at sixty."

"Then why can't you vote? Is it because you're a Shaker?"

"No. It's account of I can't read or write. When a man cannot do those things, people think his head is weak. Even when he's proved his back is strong."

"Who decides?"

"Men who look at me and do not take me for what I be. Men who only see me make my mark, my X, when I can't sign my name. They can't see how I true a beam to build our barn, or see that the rows of corn in my field are straight as fences. They just see me walk the street in Learning in clothes made me by my own woman. They do not care that my coat is sturdy and keeps me warm. They'll not care that I owe no debt, and that I am beholding to no man."

"Is that why you can't vote, Papa?"

"Yes, boy. That's the reason."

"Doesn't it make you heartsick?"

"No. I take what I am. We are Plain People, your mother and aunt, and your sisters, you and me. We live the Book of Shaker. We are not worldly people, and we suffer the less for not paining with worldly wants and wishes. I am not heartsick, because I am rich and they are poor."

"We're not rich, Papa. We're . . . "

"Yes we are, boy. We have one another to fend to, and this land to tend. And one day we'll own it outright. We have Solomon here to wind up a capstan and help us haul our burdens. And look here, he's almost done pulling that cratch where we want it pulled to. We have Daisy's hot milk. We got rain to wash up with, to get the grime off us. We can look at sundown and see it all, so that it wets the eye and hastens the heart. We hear all the music that's in the wind, so much music that it itches my foot to start tapping. Just like a fiddle."

"Maybe so, Papa. But it seems to me what we have most is dirt and work."

"True enough. But it be *our* dirt, Rob. This land

will be all ours, in just a few more year. As to the work, what matters is that we have the back to do it. Some days I get the notion that I can't knife even one more of Clay Sander's pigs. Yet I always do, 'cause it's got to be done. It's my mission."

"Papa, is that the mission they preach on at Meeting?"

"It is. And every man must face his own mission. Mine is pigs. And I be thankful to be in the picture."

"What picture?"

"The picture of Vermont, boy. Do you know what makes Vermont a good state?"

"No."

"It's simple as beans. Here in this state we know just two things. We can turn grass into milk and corn into hogs."

"I guess that's as true as a taproot."

"Truer."

Walking his circle, Solomon snorted as if to say he blessed the whole business.

"They sure is a passel of corn and meadow land in these parts," I said. "If'n we turn all this and all that to milk and hogs, blessed if we'd ever keep up with it. Or just keep it in sight."

"Probably wouldn't, be we all dreamers like you. Now old Solomon's a dreamer, too. But yet he walks his circle. And just look how he's drug that corn cratch. Plenty far."

I couldn't believe it. Just while Papa and me were talking, Solomon drug that old corn crib into place and moved it a ways that was twice as long as Papa was tall. And then Papa added some fresh-cut timbers to winter-tight the cratch for Pinky.

"Papa?"

"Yup."

"You using fresh wood?"

"Yup."

"Don't it got to season before you build with it?"

"Indoors, yes. But you can wood up a wall to stand outdoors and fresh wood will season itself."

With a handturn, Papa sunk holes into the fresh planks at both ends, and into the old wood beyond. In each hole he used a mallet to pound in a trunnel peg of white oak that he had soaking in linseed oil. And the sty was done.

Pinky slept in it her first night with us. So did I, because the way I figured it, she'd be lonesome in a new place and away from her big fat old ma. So together we nestled down into all the clean straw, under what was left of Mr. Tanner's old horse blanket.

With Pinky next to me that night, I guess I must have been the luckiest boy in Learning.

Chapter

5

The next day was Sunday.

Of course the four of us went to Shaker Meeting—
me and Mama, and Papa, and Aunt Carrie. We went
in the wagon, and Solomon pulled it. All the way to
Learning and all the way home. It was a real good
sunny Sunday, perfect all around. And the best part
was, I sat in Meeting where I could see Becky Tate
and she couldn't see me.

That afternoon, Pinky and I went for a walk up
on the ridge that parts our land from Mr. Tanner's.
We didn't go too near the spot where old Apron and
I met up. I don't hanker to ever see that place right
away quick; and if it's never, you won't hear a howl
from me.

One nice thing about April, there were little rivers
about everywhere. Where the spruce cover was thick,
you could still see a patch of snow here or there,

and the ground was still hard as winter. But only in spots. Most of the land lay open to sun; and it was soft and brown, ready to be mated with seed.

Pinky rooted around in the leaves and found her very first butternut, left over from fall. She sniffed it a while with her little pink nose, and then she tried to crack it with her teeth. She couldn't do it, but it sure wasn't from lack of trying. So I put the butternut on a flat rock, and smashed it with another stone. And fed the meat of the butternut to Pinky. We looked around for more, and found a few. Pinky seemed to take to them, because each time I'd stop to crack one, she'd almost always have her nose in the way of the rock.

One of the tiny rivers was only about as wide as my hand, but the current was swift. It was a perfect spot to build what I liked to build every spring.

"Pinky," I said, "you ever see a flutterwheel? Well, I'm going to make one, so you watch real close and careful."

I found two tiny fork-sticks, which I pushed into the mud (fork up) on both sides of the stream. Then from one fork to the other I put a basswood axle, with a dab of mud in the crotch of both forks to grease its turning. All was needed then were three or four paddles that I stuck into the axle. By pushing the two fork-sticks deeper into the mud until the water touched the paddle blades, the flutterwheel finally turned. The strong current of the tiny creek made it turn round and round.

Pinky watched it for a moment or two, but didn't find it near as comely as butternuts.

She sure was my pig. As I lay on the ground on a brown carpet of spruce needles, Pinky would wander off by herself. But never very far. No farther than you could kick a barrel with just one good kick. (The barrel on its side and rolling.) One time she went a little farther from me. And a big black crow over her head in a hickory tree let out a bark that made her jump and squeal like she'd been stuck. She come running to me like the Fallen Angel was after her. She never stopped squealing until she was in my arms, with her slobber all over me. I let her feel the warm of my shirt next to her. She was my pig.

Only minutes after the crow spooked her, she was wading in the water not too far from where the flutterwheel was turning. She came close to stepping on a frog. And when it jumped, so did she. You couldn't tell which one was more scared of the other, the frog or Pinky. All the frog took was just one jump, and set there. Like he was waiting for her.

He didn't wait long. Pinky got her gumption up in no time and went close enough to smell him. This time when he jumped, she pulled back a bit. But didn't spook. Not Pinky. I guess she knew he wasn't anything more than a little old hopfrog and that he wasn't anything to run from. She kept right on chasing him, and he kept right on leaping. It was fair to see.

He got so busy keeping away from Pinky that he made a big misdo. He plumb forgot about that old black crow that was sitting up above, just watching that game of tag. It didn't take that wise old bird long to see himself a meal. He dropped out of that hickory tree like a big black stone, landed with his feet splashing the water, and took one sharp clear peck at that frog. Hit him dead-center.

By the time Pinky jumped away, I saw the last of Mr. Frog. He just disappeared with his white belly up, right into the beak and the gullet of that crow. He tasted good, you can bet. I'd ate the legs off a big fat bullfrog on many a summer, so I know. Just like chicken, only you got to skin 'em first. Unless you skin 'em, they're real slimy. And you can only eat the hind legs. The front ones you just have to throw to the chickens.

Funny thing about that. I was cleaning a mess

of frogs one time, with Papa. I said: "Papa, ain't it a caution that we can only eat two legs off a frog, 'stead of four."

And he said: "Rob, here's what you do. You catch a real big bullfrog and make friends with him. And teach him to jump backwards. That'll make his front legs big as the hind."

You know, I actually tried it. I went to the sump the next day and caught me a bullfrog and spent the better part of a morning trying to learn that old frog to jump backwards, so he'd build up his front legs. But you think he'd do it? Not even once. Papa wasn't one to smile every year, but he sure did then.

Before I knew it, there I was, telling that frog story to Pinky. I don't know whether she found it as mirthful as Papa, but she seemed to enjoy it some.

"Pink," I said, "how about it? You want a frog for supper?"

She just looked at me with her funny little eyes, which could of meant yes. So we left the flutter-wheel turning and come down off the ridge, heading for the sump. It was the same swale hole that I latched the frog that I never learned to jump backwards. Maybe they'd be more and I could give Pinky a taste of froglegs.

We got to the sump okay, and started to turn over a few rocks looking for frogs. But there just didn't seem to be many around. Or any. Pinky watched me wading around looking among the rocks and marshgrass, so she thought she'd try her luck. Poking her little pink snout down between two stones at water's edge, she found something on the very first try. It was somebody who could jump backwards all right, but it weren't no frog.

She squealed! 'Cuz clinging to her nose was one powerful looking crawdad. In school, Miss Malcolm calls 'em a crayfish, but if one ever gets hold of your toe, it sure feels a lot more like a crawdad. And that old crawdad on Pinky's nose was really giving her what for. I pulled it off, and threw it back in the pond. But she kept squealing. I reckoned it gave her snout a good pinch.

From high on the ridge, Pinky and I could look down and see Mr. Tanner's farm. It sure looked prosperous next to ours. The barn was long and white-painted, and there were white fences along the lanes.

On the near side of the big white house was a small meadow. That was where we could see Apron and her two bull calves. Just a look at that big Holstein made my arm hurt. The stitches were still in it, and I guessed they'd be there until Hell froze and got hauled to the ice house. If Mama had any plan to remove her sewing, she sure hadn't told it unto me. I didn't bring it up, and wasn't going to. Just in case those stitches hurt half as much coming out as they did going in. I couldn't say for sure just how you took thread out of somebody's arm, but it would probably mean some cuting. And I wasn't about to step forward for another dose of that.

It was good to look down from the high and lonely and see Bob and Bib tagging along after Apron. Bob was the one named after me. My real name was Robert Peck, but lots of times I got called Bob. That's what Jacob Henry called me.

I was named after Robert Rogers, who was quite a man with the Indians in these parts. He's dead now. But there was a time when there wasn't an Iroquois in Vermont or in New York State that didn't hear the name of Major Robert Rogers and start to fearing. Some said he was a Shaker, born and bred. Just like Papa and just like me. But he didn't wear Shaker clothes. He wore Indian clothes most of the time, Robert Rogers did. He wore buckskin shirts and trousers; and no stockings, people said.

Major Robert Rogers was a very famous man. So famous that if you row crosslake to Ticonderoga, there's a big rock slide named after him. Indians were chasing him along the shoulder that's west of Lake George, and Robert Rogers slid down that slide to escape. That's how he got away. That's why he's so famous, according to Miss Malcolm.

"Pinky," I said, "do you know I was named after Major Robert Rogers, and that he was a Shaker just like me and you?"

Be it if Pinky was at all brightened to knowing that, she sure hid it good. She just kept rooting around in the ferns and not finding a thing. So I just kept saying to her about Robert Rogers.

"That's how he got away, Pinky. 'Course from everything I've heard and read in history books, Robert Rogers didn't have to run from the Indians at all. He could of turned and fought 'em off one by one, and killed every last one of them. He could of pushed 'em all right down that rock. Rogers Rock, it's called."

When my grandfather was still alive, I told him about Robert Rogers and all. And I said how much Major Robert Rogers hated Indians. And that's when Grampa said that he didn't hate them all. Because a number of Indian women in these parts had children that looked a bit like they was sired by Robert Rogers. They all favored him some.

Anyhow, he sure seemed to be a regular guy. So I was real proud to carry his name.

"Come on, Pinky," I said. "It's getting close to

chore time. I got to feed you and Daisy and Solomon. And if'n I'm not to home come chore time, Hell won't have it. Papa gets mighty stirred up over that. Right he should. Chores are my mission, not his."

I ran down off the ridge toward our farm as fast as I could, just to see if my pig could keep up with me. She could. I ran all the way across the North meadow, clear to the crick. And even there I didn't stop. I just jumped it. Sailed through the air and landed yonder. Pinky didn't jump from one bank to another. But she sure waded it fast as fury. Splashed right through and made all the silver jump up around her hoofs.

"Come quick," said Mama, who was standing at the barn door. Just inside was a nest in the hay, right next to the warm wall near Daisy. Down in the hay was our barn cat, Miss Sarah, and three of the prettiest kittens you'd see anywhere. One was calico like her. (And if it lived it would be a female too. Male calicoes die.) Another one was a tiger buff, and it was easy the biggest. The third one was almost all white with buff colored markings on its back and rear leg. They was a trio to behold.

Miss Sarah was real happy about it too. She lay there purring and purring and purring, like her motor was running and wouldn't stop. And those three kittens with their wet milky noses all buried into her belly, all sucking away to beat mercy.

"Look, Pinky," I said, lifting her up so she could see Miss Sarah and her litter.

"No matter how many times a barn cat has her kits," Mama said, "it's always a wondrous thing to see."

Chapter

6

June come. I sure was happy as today was the last day of school.

It was hot that afternoon. But I came racing home with my final report card all folded up in my pocket. The weather was dry as dust, and I was glad to be walking across pasture on the soft green meadowland, instead of kicking rocks the long way round which was by the dirt road.

Way off to my right side, a wagon was coming down the long hill, headed for town. I didn't know the team or the driver. As the wagon moved along the dirt road, it blowed up clouds of dust that seemed to hang in the air behind it. Looked like the wagon was chased by a long dusty-gray snake. The driver had his coat took off, riding in his shirt with his sleeves rolled up. It looked like Isadore Crookshank who sat the seat, but I couldn't tell for sure.

I watched the wagon until it went out of sight around a roadbend. And soon the snake had gone, too. It was like the wagon hadn't passed by at all.

From a quarter mile away I could see the corn cratch that Solomon moved with the capstan. And its new boards from one end to the other, like stripes, to fill in what used to be the open space between slats. Closer, I could see Pinky moving about, chasing one of the chickens.

"Pinky," I yelled. But she was too far away to hear. So I ran again. But not too far, as it sure was a hot day for June.

Now that I was near, I called to Pinky again. This time she heard, and come to meet me. Boy! She was growing. I'd had her just ten weeks and already she was about my size. I lay on my back on the grass so she could come up to me and I could see her face. It always looked to me like she was smiling. In fact, I know she was. Lots of things smile, like a flower to the sun. And one thing sure. I knew that just like I could smile to see Pinky, she sure could smile to see me.

I got up, running toward the house. Pinky followed, but not as fast as when she was tiny. Her weight gain was good, but it slowed her down some. Just as we got to the fence, I saw Mama on the front stoop, waving for me to come up to the house. I'd hoped she hadn't took notice of me rolling on the meadowgrass in my school clothes.

"Rob," she said, as I came in the house, "look who's here."

There she was, sitting in our good chair, and wearing one of her big dresses with all the colorful flowers on it, and smelling so good with perfume that it almost made me sick. There she was, Aunt Matty.

She lived in town, in Learning. Once a month or so, she'd come to pay call on Mama. She wasn't my real aunt, like Aunt Carrie. But I guess she was a distant cousin twice moved; which to go along with my reckoning means that she used to live in two other places before she moved to Learning. Anyhow, she wasn't my real aunt. Just a friend of Mama and Aunt Carrie, so that they got out the good cups to drink tea out of. But I called her Aunt Matty. Or sometimes Auntie Matt. Her real name was Martha Plover.

"Hello, Aunt Matty."

"Well, look at the size of you. You're growing like a weed." Aunt Matty always said that, and yet it always made me feel good.

"Thank you," I said.

I should have excused myself right then and there, and changed my clothes for chores. But instead I made my big mistake of the day. And it

— 52 —

could of been my big mistake of the whole darn summer.

Like a fool, I pulled out my report card.

I showed it to Mama and to Aunt Carrie. They couldn't read hardly at all, but they knew what an A looked like. I'd got A in geography, spelling, reading, arithmetic, and history. The only other mark I got was a D in English, which I didn't bother to point out. So when Mama and Aunt Carrie saw all them A's they said I was a good boy.

The trouble kicked up when I showed my report card to Aunt Matty. She could read. But as it turned out, she couldn't read the letter A, no matter how many she saw. All she could read was D, where I got a D in English.

"You got D in English!"

The way Aunt Matty took on, it must have been the first D anybody ever got, because it sure gave her the vapors. I thought she was going to die from the shock of it. Like she seen a ghost. There it was. A big black D, as big and black as Miss Malcolm could make it, right there on my old report card. And it was more than poor Aunt Matty could bear. She let out a gasp, and her hand went to her throat like she was spasmed.

"D in English," she said again, to make sure that there wasn't a soul who missed it.

Well, I thought to myself, I've done it. Brung disgrace on my family's house. Appeared a D in English was so dark a deed that no one could live it down.

" 'Course it's not the end of the world," said Aunt Matty. "There *is* a remedy."

Remedy! There was a word that struck a fever. Mama had give me a spoonful of remedy for one thing or another almost every winter and spring. It made you go to the backhouse a lot. Morning, noon, and night. Sometimes twice each, and it was no picnic to have your butt burn like Hellfire.

"All he needs," said Aunt Matty to Mama and Aunt Carrie, "is a tutor."

At this, I heaved a breath of well being. I sure knew what a "tooter" was. Jacob Henry had one. It's real name was a cornet, and he played it in the school band. But what Jacob called it was his "tooter." So I was some relieved, now knowing that I weren't going to get marched to the kitchen, took by the ear, and forced to gag down a tablespoon of remedy. A cornet was bad, the way Jacob played it. But it sure beat a remedy that you had to swallow now and run after.

"Fact is," said Aunt Matty, "I will tutor him myself." That was when I busted out laughing fit to kill. Aunt Matty, big and round in her flower dresses and all her beads, was strange to look at as she was. But to see her blowing on a cornet, with her cheeks all puffed out the way Jacob's got, was too much to stand. A sight like that could lead the high school band in a parade. Auntie Matt and her silver cornet, highstepping down the main street of Learning every Four of July. It was more than ribs could take.

That's when I should of known better. Seeing me laugh was more than Aunt Matty could bear. Anyone who got a D in English had no right to joy. It was her next words that stopped the laughing for time to come.

"D in English! It's no laughing matter. Next thing it'll be an F, for Failure. And you know what that means. Expulsion. He'll be put back a grade. So there's no time to lose. I'll start to tutor him today, and right now. Come, Robert."

Up jumped Aunt Matty, grabbing me with one of her chubby hands and her big old floppy pocket-book with the other. I could tell she meant business. As she drug me into the parlor, all her bracelets were rattling as if to say so. Well, it was all right with me. If Aunt Matty wanted to play the cornet, I was partial to it.

"Grammar," she said, pushing me with some force into a hardwood ladderback chair. "That's where you're falling down. Before I married your

Uncle Hume, I was an English teacher. And that's where we're going to start. Living in this house and all its Shaker ways, it's a wonder you can talk at all. You'd get better than a D in English if you were a fearing Baptist."

That was it! That there was the time my heart almost stopped. I'd heard about the Baptists from Jacob Henry's mother. According to her, Baptists were a strange lot. They put you in water to see how holy you were. Then they ducked you under the water three times. Didn't matter a whit if you could swim or no. If you didn't come up, you got dead and your mortal soul went to Hell. But if you did come up, it was even worse. You had to be a Baptist.

And here I was, alone with one. Bless the dear old goodness there weren't a pond in our parlor. It sure would be a painful caution to have a Baptist the size of Aunt Matty hold you under. Even to think of it made me gasp for breath, and I made a throaty noise.

"You all right?" asked Aunt Matty, digging around inside her big pocketbook. She came up with a tiny whitelace hanky, not much bigger than a stamp.

"Here," she said, "blow your nose. You can't learn English with an acting sinus."

I blew!

"Now then," said Aunt Matty, as she snatched back her hanky, giving it a sick look, "we're going to have a little test on grammar. You tell me, Robert, which sentence is correct. Ready?"

"Yes'm."

"It was I who he called. It was me who he called. It was I *whom* he called. And, it was me whom he called."

I just sat there, dumb as a post. I guessed I didn't have brains enough to dump sand out a boot. If she'd asked me if'n I was Robert Peck, I don't guess I could of answered a good stout yes or no.

"Well?"

"I don't know, Auntie Matt. They all sound fair enough to me."

"Just as I suspected from the first."

"The first what?"

"It's just an expression, Rob. But it's just as I feared. You don't know grammar, because you don't know how to *diagram*."

"We haven't had that yet," I said.

" 'Course you haven't. Trouble with teachers to-day is, they don't diagram. All they think of is the Bunny Hug."

"We haven't had that either."

Aunt Matty went fishing into her big pocketbook once again. She pulled out an armload of things that she didn't want, and finally some paper and pencil.

"So," she said, writing as fast as she talked, "I am going to write out a sentence, and *you* can diagram it. Hear?"

"Yes."

"There now. *Jack hit the ball hard with Joe's yellow bat.* Let's see you diagram *that.*"

"I can't, Auntie Matt."

"I know you can't. But any schoolboy who gets a D had better learn. First off, what's the subject?"

"English."

"What?"

"English is the subject I got a D in."

Aunt Matty wiped her face with the hanky I blowed my nose into. She gave a big sigh (like Solomon when he's pulling the plow and comes to the end of a furrow) and I knew that grammar sure was a tribulation.

"Rob," she said real soft, "I used to teach English, and there was one thing I never did. Know what that was?"

"Played the cornet?"

"Not exactly. I never got angry. A good teacher does not lose her temper, no matter how stupid her pupils are."

"That's good," I said, "because in our school they sure are some dull ones."

As Aunt Matty fanned herself with the hanky, I wondered what she was thinking about. I was joyful to hear that Aunt Matty didn't get mad. An angry teacher is bad aplenty, but I didn't know how good I could fend off an angry Baptist.

Picking up the pencil, Aunt Matty started to draw some lines and circles (and a few other gee-gaws that I'd never seen before and never seen since) on the sentence about Jack. She put a zig-zag here, and a crazy elbow joint there. There was ovals and squiggles all over the paper. It was the fanciest thing I ever saw. The part about Jack was still in sight, but now it had arms and legs that thrashed out in six directions. It looked to me like a hill of barb-wire. And the worse it got, the prouder Aunt Matty was of it.

"Behold!" she said at last, trying to pry loose the pencil from her own fingers. "*That* is a diagram!"

I wasn't about to make sport of it. Aunt Carrie always said that only the foolish defy the Dark Spirits. I didn't know the truth of it, but years back in the town of Learning, somebody had come across an old woman who was a witch. She'd just look at a barn and it'd burn to cinders. She could dry up a creek with one crack of her knuckles. And sour your cow's milk before it bubbled in the pail. One look from that old witch, they said, would mildew silage and peel paint. Must have been a Baptist.

"Gee, Aunt Matty," I said. "I ought to get A in English now for certain."

"Here," she said, handing me the paper that she'd sweated over like it was canning. "Take it up to your room and pin it on the wall."

She pushed the paper to my hand, and I felt the unholy touch of it all the way upstairs and down.

"Did you thank Aunt Matty?" my mama asked me. "Can't forget manners."

"Thank you, Aunt Matty. Now I got to do chores. If'n it don't get done, they'll be a nevermind of fuss 'tween I and Papa."

I was careful not to slam the door. Just outside, Pinky was waiting for me, and we raced each other to the barnyard fence. And just as I took leave of the house, I heard all of Aunt Matty's bracelets go rattling, and I heard mama say:

"How was the first lesson?"

"Next time," said Aunt Matty, "I'll teach the pig."

Chapter

7

Up on the ridge north from our house, it was open field. You could walk for most of a mile before reaching the woods.

The grass was high now. And seeing as I'd worked all day on the hay wagon with Papa, it sure felt good just to know that evening chores were done, and I could lie on my back in the soft grass and do nothing except wait for evening.

Pinky was with me, and she was lying down too. Even though she hadn't put in a lick of work all day. But there she was, a mound of white pig in a whole field of purple clover and kickweed. Here and there was a stand of wild paintbrush. Most of it yellow, and some red. It didn't seem to want to mix with the clover, and it just kept to its own kind.

The whole hillside was purple clover; and in the early sundown, it looked more purple than I'd ever see it. Pinky was rolling in it. Over and back, over and back. I knew it felt good to her, because I was lying in it myself, and the clover felt right and good to me. The clover was getting ripe now, and you could take a big red-purple ball of it in your hand, and pull out the flower shoots. They were good to suck, and tasted just as sweet as the bee honey that was made from them.

Drawing one between my front teeth, I squeezed the sugary nectar into my mouth and spit out the pulp. It sure tasted good. I'd tried to get Pinky to taste some, but I guess that pigs just don't cotton to clover none.

Just overhead, I could see a hawk drawing a circle in the sky. He was low for a hawk, and he must of just left his nest on the ridge and was making his first circle of evening flight. He went higher, with little moving of his wings. As he passed over us, I could see the red of his tail—like a torch against the softer colors of his underbody.

He went up, up, up. His circles were wider as he drifted south over the open meadowland of our farm. So high that he was only a dark speck with wings. The clouds above him were orange now. Like when Mama poured peach juice on the large curds of white potcheese. At the western-most turn of his circle, I almost lost him in the sundown.

But now he was returning. I wanted him to come

back so as I could watch him circle. As the tiny speck of him passed over my head, he stopped. For an instant he didn't fly at all, and just appeared to be pasted against a cloud, not moving. Then he got bigger, and bigger. I couldn't see any wings, as he was falling fast as a stone. I sat up in the clover to watch his dive, and for a minute I thought he was coming down for me.

I knew a hawk wouldn't bother me none, so I sure knew it weren't me that hawk was hunting. And down he came; down, down, down. Not moving his wings at all, like they was pegged to his sides and he couldn't brake his fall. He was going to hit the ground for sure, and I jumped on my feet to see it.

Whump! The hawk hit only a few rods from where I was standing in the clover. Just the yonder side of a juniper bush where the clover wasn't nearby at all, and where it once had been open meadowland for pasture. He hit something as big as he was, pretty near. And whatever it was, it was thrashing about on the ground. Seeing his talons were buried in its fur, the hawk was being whipped through that juniper bush for fair. But all he had to do was hang on, and drive his talons into the heart or lungs.

Then I heard the cry. Full of pity it was, and it even made Pinky get to her feet. I'd only heard it once before, a rabbit's deathcry, and it don't forget very easy. Like a newborn baby, that's the sort of noise it is. Maybe even a call for help, for somebody to come and end its hurting. It's the only cry that a rabbit makes its whole life long, just that one death-cry and it's all over.

The cottontail rabbit had stopped kicking; and the hawk was resting after the struggle, probably trying to get his breath back. So I didn't move. Pinky either. We both stood stock still, up to our knees in that clover like we was hitched. That old hawk saw us, you can wager on that. He saw us for certain sure, but it didn't mean spit to him.

I started to move forward real slow through the stand of clover, toward the hawk. Trying to keep the juniper bush 'tween the two of us, and hoping that big white pig didn't come crashing along to see what was up. Took about three steps and that was all. Mr. Hawk snapped those big wings out and whipped 'em fast, so off he went. I could tell that rabbit was dead, the way it hung all loose in the talons of that old redtail. The hawk went off and away from us, flying low and close to ground until his speed was such as he could climb. To him that rabbit must of been a burden and a half, but it sure was going to be a hot meal.

The grass whipped on my legs as I ran after him, fast as I could. So I could see where on that ridge his nest was that I knew he'd circle back to.

Pinky didn't want to miss a trick, so she was right at my heels. But I lost sight of the hawk. He just plain melted over a hilltop and out of sight. I sure would of wanted to see his nest. And to see him tear up that fresh rabbit and feed his little ones. I bet soon as he landed at his nest with his kill, all his brood had their beaks open, wanting to get some hunks of warm rabbit down their gullet.

Any rabbit we ever shot, Papa always rubbed its belly hair up the wrong way, to see if it was healthy. If he felt bumps on the belly, then he'd bury it because of it being down with rabies. If it was sound, it was pie.

It made me hungry just to study on it. I'd tasted rabbit plenty of times myself, and it was better than goose. Mama was one good cook when it come to tanning a rabbit in her oven. There wasn't one mighty thing that either Papa or me could rifle that Mama couldn't put in the pot.

So if those young hawk nestings went after that rabbit meat, it was only because they got to it ahead of me. I didn't know if Pinky would like rabbit or no. But all pigs are meat-eaters. Sure ought to be with forty-four teeth, Papa said. That was more teeth than I got. So maybe old Pinky would of eat rabbit. All I know is, a sow hog will eat her brood if she's not fed right. That what Papa says.

I sure fed Pinky good. Just to make sure she

got to grow right, I give her as much corn, wheat, barley, rye, oats, and sorghum as I could work out of Papa or Mr. Tanner. She also got some of Daisy's good fresh milk. Any time I went fishing, she got fish. And all the soybean meal and alfalfa I could muster. Mama said, "Rob, you feed that pig better'n you feed yourself." I guessed it was true. She was my pig. Mine. And I was going to be dogged if she'd eat improper.

That was just food. She drunk about ten pounds a day of water. And like Solomon and Daisy, she liked her water cold and fresh. I was at Jacob Henry's once and he was watering the stock. They had a horse and a cow, and only one bucket, so Jacob always had to water the horse first. Because a cow will drink after a horse, but no horse will drink after a cow. And a cow'll drink three pails to one for a horse. But the horse got to drink first.

I kept a record of how much I fed Pinky, and wrote it all down up in my bedroom. The way I had it figured, for every three hundred fifty pounds of feed I give, she ought weight-gain a hundred. As I was setting there in the clover, chewing on a juniper berry, Pinky come over and rub against me. And it was some rub, because she sure was growing. I'd a give up pie for breakfast if I could of growed like she growed.

"Pinky," I said, "you get took good care of. You got shelter and shade, and your crib is well drained. There's always dry straw for you to sleep on, and the sump hole by the brook for mud to roll in. I even wet down the yard for you so the dust don't creep in your nose."

She snorted. I knew she wasn't saying thank you or anything, but it sure was fun to pretend so.

"You're welcome, Pink. And I'm going to keep right on taking care of you proper. Because do you know what you aim to be? You ain't going to be pork. No, missy. You're going to be a brood sow, and have a very long life. You get to be sized good, and heat up like a sow pig ought to, and we're going to breed you to Mr. Tanner's boar. Just wait until you see Samson. He's about the best breeding boar in Learning, according to Papa. You and Samson are going to get mounted and mated, and the first litter ought to be at least eight. And after that, ten."

All this here talk of motherhood didn't seem to take to Pinky. She moved away from me and snapped at a bee.

"Bee," I said, "you must be the last one out tonight. Better get home to your tree. It's getting dark."

The whole sky was pink and peaches. Just looking up at it made you feel clean, even if you worked all day. We walked down the hill together; Pinky looking close to the ground the way she always did, and me watching the sundown. The old sun just seem to back off and leave us be.

We got home, and I penned Pinky up for the night, and gave her an extra big goodnight hug. I was walking back toward the house and met Papa coming to the barn. One of the kittens was there too, and I picked her up and carried her. The tiny claws dug into my shoulder, right through my shirt, until I held her close to make her fret no more of falling.

Papa had been mending a harness trace for Mr. Sander, and I waited while he slowly put all his tools away, each to its proper bed on the wall of the tackroom. Then we went outside and sat on a bench on the westerly side of the barn, me still holding the kitten on my lap, and we watched the sun go down. The pink become purple, and the purple turned to what Mama called a Shaker gray.

"Papa," I said, "of all the things in the world to see, I reckon the heavens at sundown has got to be my favorite sight. How about you?"

"The sky's a good place to look," he said. "And I got a notion it's a good place to go."

Chapter
8

I didn't know what time it was, and I sure didn't care. Not in the center of night, and raining as hard as it was raining.

The thunder was crashing, too. Water was coming in my window, so I swung it shut. My window looked to the barn, and even through the rain I could see the yellow of a lantern deep inside the shed.

Voices were downstairs. I could hear Mama and Aunt Carrie, and another voice. A woman that I didn't know was talking. I was about to get back under the quilt, but decided not. Instead I went to the nook at the stairtop and listened. Then I recognized the voice. It's was Mrs. Hillman from up the road. She was standing at the front door, carrying a lantern.

Mama and Aunt Carrie were trying to ask her into

the house. Something was said about a hot cup of tea, but I didn't hear all of it on account it rained so blessed hard. Mrs. Hillman finally come in; and they got the door shut, which improved the listening.

"He's gone," said Mrs. Hillman. "Sebring's gone. I heard him take the team and go in the night, and don't think I don't know where. Spade and all, I saw him go. He picked a night like this so nobody'd see him rile her grave. I know."

Again there was talk of tea, and I could hear cups against saucers somewhere back in the kitchen.

"That Letty Phelps, your husband's kin. She hired out to us, when I was poorly years back. I know. I could see from out my bedroom glass. See her going to the barn to be with him. And then the trouble, the borning and the dying."

Papa come in from outside, shaking his slicker. I saw him drop it on the drainboard near the sink, and turn. I just got back in bed when I heard him call.

"Rob, get yourself up and dressed and hitch up the ox to the long wagon."

I got dressed so fast my trousers were on front side back, and it felt sort of queer. But I pulled on my boots with no socks and run downstairs and out to the shed. With all the racket, both Solomon and Daisy were wide awake. Maybe even wondering like I was as to what was up and afoot.

I got Solomon hitched up. It was all I could do to get the yoke on him. First time I'd ever done it alone. I wanted to go back to the house to learn what was happening. My stomach felt sort of vacant and I had the shakes. Just as I was about to make a dash for the house through the rain, I saw Papa coming with a bigger lantern and the shotgun.

Before I could ask what was astir or where were we going, Papa threw me up on the wagon seat and covered me with an old buffalo robe. He sat close.

"Hold the lantern, boy."

He poked the long wand to Solomon's rump and the wagon lurched out into the rain and the pitch black. I kept looking back through the mist toward our house, wanting to be home in bed. The yellow window got smaller and smaller and I was wondering where we were headed.

"There's talk about a new county road," Papa yelled to me in the raining, "and they say it's wide enough to cut the corner of the churchyard at the Meeting House."

"Is that where we be going, Papa?"

"That's where."

"Why?"

"We don't let Sebring Hillman desecrate what's ours that's buried there."

"What's desecrate?"

"Dig up."

So we were headed for a graveyard. That much I knew. What Mr. Hillman was fixing to dig up, or why, was beyond wondering. I was cold and wet and wanted to go to sleep.

"Sit close," said Papa. "And mind you don't drop that lantern."

Twice we had to get down and push the wagon through mud. It frosted the wheels like they was cake, and it sucked at your boots. Made you feel you were standing in syrup.

We got to Learning, and the town was all asleep in the rain. We rounded the corner at the General Store and went toward Meeting. There was no lantern aglow in the churchyard. But we could hear his shovel hitting wood. It sure sounded lonely. Solomon stopped at the cemetery gate, and we went in on foot. We moved toward where Sebring Hillman was working, and the ring of light from our lantern took him in its circle. Looking up from the hole he was brown with dirt.

"Who's there?" he said.

"Neighbors, Seeb," said Papa. "It's Haven Peck and son Robert. And we come to take you on home."

"Not 'til this work is done. And the sin and trouble is ended for all to see and all to know."

"She's my kin," said Papa. "And I don't aim to see kin dug up in the cover of nightfall. Best you drop your shovel."

I held the heavy wet buffalo robe around me tight as I could. Papa held the gun in the crook of his arm, muzzle down. Hillman come up out of the hole, covered with mud, but holding the shovel high. His face was wet with raining. He was looking up both the barrel holes of Papa's gun.

"You got a gun," he said, and his voice was an illness.

"It's for varmits," Papa said, "not for neighbors."

"I don't purpose to disturb the box that Letty rests in," he said. "And that's Gospel."

"It's best," Papa said.

Papa took a shovel out of our wagon and the two men poked at the mud. They found a smaller box, and lifted it up. They replaced the earth as it was before. The headstone said PHELPS, and that wasn't touched.

"By rights," said Papa, "that child of hers could go in our orchard plot."

This was when Sebring Hillman lifted up the

small box and held it close to his chest. He was a big man and he needed no help for it. He just stood there, yelling in the raining.

"She don't have folks. They left town after she drown this child, then hung herself. I can't undo what's already been did. But the little girl is mine. You hear me, Haven? This child is mine, and I claim it soul and dust."

"You'll wake the town," Papa said.

"Yes, and I hope to do just that. I never did step forward back then. But by damn I claim it now. I own up. This little girl is mine. She's . . . she's Hillman's claim!"

"So be it," said Papa. "Let's get our young ones home and rested proper."

We watched as Mr. Hillman carried the small coffin to where his wagon and team stood hid behind the Meeting House. We followed close along so as he'd have light to see. He tied the coffin firm with rope, and was about to mount the seat. He was wet through.

"You don't have a slicker," Papa said, almost like asking.

"No."

"Tie your team behind our wagon, and ride with us," Papa said. "We got a slicker and robe."

"I will."

We were about halfway home, and I was sitting the wagon bench between Papa and Mr. Hillman. Next to the two of them it was warm and dark, and I could smell the wet musty smell of the buffalo robe. Mr. Hillman held the lantern. Ahead of us the light showed on Solomon's mighty backside as he moved into the darkness, following the road up from town and back home.

"Haven?" I heard Hillman speak.

"Yup."

"I'm sorry about your cousin Letty. And about the digging."

"It's over and done," Papa said. "And all I want right now is breakfast."

"And I."

"Your wife is at our place."

"May? May's at your place? Then that's how you come to town."

"That's how."

"She's a good woman, May."

"Are we home, Papa?" I said.

"Near."

"I want breakfast, too."

"So do I, boy," said Sebring Hillman. "I want so much breakfast it'll bust britches and crack floors. I never felt so good in a long time."

"Mr. Hillman?"

"Sure enough."

"Is that really your little girl in the coffin?"

"It is, Robert. And if it's all right with you and your pa, I'm going to bury her in Hillman land. With a Hillman name."

"I guess that's proper," I said, and sort of went off to sleep.

By the time we turned into our own lane and got to the house, the rain had stopped. And it was sunup to the east. When Papa lifted me down from the wagon seat, I opened my eyes. There was a light in the kitchen, and Papa said, "There's coffee on."

"That'll be good," said Hillman.

I went to the house with Mr. Hillman while Papa put Solomon in the barn. We went to the kitchen door, because of the mud. He took off my boots, and I went inside to the kitchen. Hillman said he was too muddy and wet. Mrs. Hillman was sitting in the kitchen. She looked at her husband but no word passed. Mama handed Mr. Hillman a mug of hot coffee.

"Thank you, Sister," he said.

Mama took a good look at me, yanked me into the pantry, and stripped me down to my skin. She rubbed me dry with a flour sack until I thought all my hide was coming off. Then she wrapped me up in a blanket that she took out of the warming oven over the stove, and gave me a big spoonful of hot honey.

"You look like a potato dug up on a rainy day," Mama said.

Going through the kitchen on my way upstairs, I saw Mr. Hillman still standing on the kitchen porch, holding the white mug of coffee in both hands. He drank every drop. He was still wet with mud.

"Let's go home, May," he said to his wife. They went outside, untied their team, and headed uproad to home.

Behind them rode a baby's coffin.

Chapter

9

I was just outside the kitchen window, trying to give Pinky a bath. Not really listening.

But I could hear Aunt Carrie and Mama in the pantry, and they seemed to be het up over something that didn't make any sense to me one way or the other. Aunt Carrie seemed to have most of the ache and distress on her side.

"It's shameful," she said.

Then I could hear some pie tins rattle, and I figured it was Aunt Carrie who done it, as a snit.

"Shameful. Them two living under the same roof, without benefit of clergy. You know well as I what's going on in that house, right under our very noses."

"Maybe," said Mama, "our noses are where they shouldn't be."

"You heard Matty say it, when she was here the other day."

"Matty says more than her prayers."

"Right under our noses, all that sin."

"Carrie, you know well as I that the Widow Bascom and her hired man ain't living under our noses. They're near a mile down road."

"Too close for comfort."

"Maybe it's time that Widow Bascom took some comfort, and him too."

"It's shameful. And to think of Vernal Bascom, not yet cold in his grave. Poor soul."

"Carrie, you know weller than I that Vernal Bascom he's been gone two maybe three year."

"Didn't take *her* long to hire a man."

"Haven says he's a worker. And I say the Bascom place never looked better. She couldn't of done it alone, run that farm. Life ain't easy for a widow woman."

"Easy's the word for her."

"What goes on under a neighbor's quilt is nought to me," said Mama.

"Plenty goes on. He's a big strapper of a man, and I'll wager he's more than a year riper than she be."

"You seen him?"

"No."

"You just hear it from Matty."

"Hume told Matty that he was driving by the Bascom place, late one night last week, and he heard laughing. And there weren't a light burning in the whole house."

"Sometimes that's the way of it," said Mama.

"Way of what?"

"Often there's lots to laugh at in the dark."

"Hume heard it all."

"I bet he slowed his horse to listen."

"Hume's a decent man," said Aunt Carrie.

"Decent and dull. They'd be little to laugh at in the dark with him."

"Shame."

"I say if Hume ever smiled he'd break his legs."

"Hume heard what he heard," said Carrie. "He told Matty it was such a noise and carrying on that he wanted to whip his horse all the way to the churchyard and wake up Vernal."

"Vernal Bascom wasn't that much awake even when he was standing up. Now that he rests in peace, why don't Hume just let him rest."

"Amen."

"I can see it," said Mama.

"See what?"

"I can just see Hume Plover in the churchyard whispering to Vernal. Hume never spoke to him all the time he was alive. Now he's at rest, and Hume wants to spark up a chat."

"You just go on and on."

"That I do, Miss Carrie. There's little enough to snicker at in this old world. And to see Hume Plover whipping up his horse to talk to the dead is enough to give me the all overs. I just wish Widow Bascom and her hired hand could see it, too." Mama was laughing.

"Shameful."

"And if Iris Bascom and her man giggle in the dark, they can have my blessing for whatever it's worth."

As I sat there on the bench outside, trying to rub the clay mud off Pinky, I got to thinking about my own run-in with Widow Bascom.

It was after Vernal passed on, and she was living alone. Me and Jacob Henry had run through her strawberry patch and across her backyard. She come out with a broom so fast, we didn't ever know how she got us cornered. We both got whacked so heavy that neither one of us took a step for a week without weeping. She caught me in the shin so hard, it gave me a welt.

I touched the place on my leg where Widow Bascom's broom handle landed. The scar of that welt was still there. Needless to say, Jacob never told his mother about it. I sure never told Mama. Papa either. I'd probably got a second birching. Papa didn't take too kind to trespass.

That was just the first time I had do with Mrs. Bascom. The second time was just day before yesterday. I was walking by her place on the dirt road (not through her damn strawberries) and she come out the house and called to me.

"Morning," she said.

"Morning, Mrs. Bascom," I said, but I sure didn't stop to say it.

"These flower pots are so heavy and all," she'd said. "I don't reckon you'd help me tug a few."

I looked good and hard for that broom of hers that was ten foot long and made of iron. Didn't see it, so I climbed the stairs and got close. She was smiling.

"Flower pots full of dirt are such pesky things," she said. "No way to carry one except to tug."

"I can lift one," I said, picking up a big pot.

"My," she said, "you're such a strong boy."

"I can yoke our ox by myself, too," I said. If she wanted to be friendly, I was game. It sure beat a brooming. So I helped her move the flower pots. In the Book of Shaker it says to do a good turn and neighbor well. Besides, it wasn't chore time yet, and I could spare the work.

"Thank you," she said to me after we got the pots moved into a sunny spot. I never saw so many flowers, all of 'em pretty. Sort of like Mrs. Bascom.

"Welcome," I said.

"Just you wait," she said, and ran into the house. In no time she was back with a glass of buttermilk and a generous plate of gingersnaps, as big as moons.

"Here," she said, "I bet you're hungry."

"I'm always hungry," I said, "because I got a tapeworm."

"A tapeworm? You don't."

"No, I don't suspect I do. I seen a pig with worms once. Ugly as sin. Excuse me. I didn't mean to say that."

I was drinking the good cool buttermilk and helping myself to plenty more gingersnaps, when I looked up at a man.

"This here is Ira," she said. "He's my new hired hand."

"How do," I said, trying not to choke on a gingersnap. He sure was big.

"How do," he said. "I'm Ira Long."

"I'm Robert Peck."

"Haven Peck's boy," said Mrs. Bascom.

We shook hands, and Ira helped himself to a handful of gingersnaps. He ate about five on the first bite.

"Say," he said, "you the boy who helped bring Ben Tanner's cow to calf? And pulled a goiter?"

"Yes."

"That was a thing you done, Rob."

"Thank you, sir."

"I seen them bull calves. Twins."

"Bob and Bib," I said. "The one they call Bob is named for me."

"That's an honor," said Mrs. Bascom.

"It blessed is," Ira said.

I couldn't think of anything to say so I just took another gingersnap and stuffed it into my mouth so's I wouldn't have to talk. Sticking out my cheek, it made a shelf you could of set a dish on. Ira and Mrs. Bascom looked at me and started to laugh, and I go so fussed I just turned around a couple of times. Then I started to laugh, too. I still don't know what was so all-fired funny. But it was.

"Them two young oxen," said Ira. "I hear Ben Tanner's taking 'em to Rutland Fair."

The very mention of Rutland Fair made my heart jump. Jacob Henry had gone to Rutland Fair last year, and he told me that it just wouldn't be believed. Anything that weren't at Rutland Fair just wasn't worth seeing. To hear Jacob tell it, the Fair was some spot.

"You ever been, Rob?"

"No. But I'd sure take a pride in going, with the pig I raised. Her name is Pinky. Guess when I get growed up, I'll go every year. But we can't go now."

"How come?"

"We don't have a horse, and I hear it's quite a ways away. All we got is Solomon."

"Who's that?" asked Mrs. Bascom.

"Solomon's our ox. He's slow. But he's big and strong and wise, like King Solomon. He's in the Bible."

"That a fact," said Ira.

"Best I be going," I said. "Thank you for the gingersnaps and the buttermilk."

"You're more than welcome, Rob," said Mrs. Bascom. "Anytime you come this way, be sure to stop for a how do."

"I will. Goodbye, Ira."

"So long, Rob."

That's what I was remembering as I sat washing up Pinky. That pig sure did get dirty. She'd even got mud in her ears. When I first got her, washing her was no trouble on account of her being so tiny and all. But now! She was getting bigger than August.

Papa come round the kitchen corner, carrying a gear for the quern. Mama had a small hand quern in the milk house, which she used to grind up meal. I turned the crank.

"You'll wash that pig away," Papa said. "Won't be nothing left of Pinky 'cept a lump of lard."

"I'm getting her clean, so I can put a ribbon on

her neck and pretend I'm taking her to Rutland."

Papa hunkered down on his heels and watched me wash Pinky. She was clean as an archangel.

"Rob?"

"Yes, sir."

"Do you think you could keep both your feet out of trouble if you was to go by yourself to Rutland?"

I couldn't talk. I knew he was funning me about going to Rutland. It weren't for real.

"Ben Tanner stopped by. He offered to take you to the Fair with him. Seems like Mrs. Bascom told Mrs. Tanner how much you wanted going. Ben asked me. He says he wants to show off them young oxen, and he wants a boy to work 'em in the ring. Said that they was too small just yet for him and that he'd feel foolish."

"Papa, is this a joke to play on me? If it is, I don't think I can take it."

"You ain't heard all, boy. Mr. Tanner says he's sending some stock up a day early. He says if you want to show Pinky, she can go too."

"Papa, please . . . "

"Now then. It's more than a week off, so I don't want to be talked to death about Rutland before you even put a foot on the Fair Grounds. Before you go, there's the hen coop that needs cleaning out. Manure's so thick in there, you got to kick a path to get eggs."

"I'll do it, Papa."

"Another thing. They won't be no spending money. Not for nothing. You hear?"

"Yes, Papa."

"Mama will make you a lunch basket that'll be breakfast, dinner, and supper. And you're to do all the Tanners ask of you. And *see* things to be done before they ask."

"Yes, Papa. I'll sure do good."

"If they judge hogs and judge oxen at the same time, your place is with Tanner's yoke and not your own pig. Promise me, boy."

"I promise, Papa. I'll do proud."

"And one more thing. It'd be right warm if you stop off and give Widow Bascom a thank you. You're beholding to her for putting the bug to Mrs. Tanner's ear."

"I will, Papa. I will. I will."

Mama was happy I was going to Rutland. Aunt Carrie wasn't so sure at first. But later that evening she said she was going to give me ten cents for the Fair; providing I didn't lose it, and didn't tell about it to Mama or Papa. It was a secret.

I sleeped out in the corn cratch with Pinky that night. She was so clean, Mama said, it would be a shame to waste it.

Before going to sleep, I put my arms around Pinky's neck and told her all about her and I on a

trip to Rutland. And how she was going to win a
blue ribbon at the showing. I told her about Widow
Bascom and Ira Long, much as I knew. And how
they giggled together in the dark.

"Pinky," I said, "having a big hired man around
like Ira may be sinful. But I say the Widow Bascom
is some improved."

Chapter

10

We'd learned in school that the city of London, England, is the largest city in the whole wide world. Maybe so. But it couldn't have been much bigger than Rutland.

Early that morning, Mama got me up. She packed my food basket so full you'd think that nobody in Vermont had ate for a week, and this was it. Papa had gone to the barn to yoke Solomon, to drive me to the Tanner place. And when Mama wasn't looking, Aunt Carrie slipped me the ten cents. She had it all knotted up in a clean white hanky and she wadded it so deep in my hip pocket, she halfway pushed my trousers down.

"Don't lose it," she whispered to my ear. Lose it? After all that wrapping, I'd be hoped to ever find it.

"It's for a ride on the merry-go-round," she said. "And if you don't want to spend it, you can squirrel it away."

To make short of it, I got breakfasted and basketed, and packed off to Tanner's. I never thought we'd get that far. Seems as though Solomon weren't near as hurried to see Rutland as I was. Maybe he already knew he wasn't going.

"Papa," I said, "tell me about Rutland."

"I never been."

Neither had I, so there really wasn't much point in talking about it. A day or two ago, Papa as much as said to Mama that if he heard the word "Rutland" three more times they was going to have to send him to Brattleboro. That's where the crazies go. I guess when they go crazy.

When I jumped out of the oxcart, and Papa was turning Solomon for home, all he said to me was one word: "Manners."

It sure wasn't far to Rutland. Not the way those dapple-gray horses of Mr. Tanner's moved that rig. They must have been barned all summer at the speed they trotted. Ben Tanner drove, and I sat between him and his wife. Tight close. But it was all Mrs. Tanner and I could do just to hold tight.

"Hang on, Bess," said Mr. Tanner, and we were off.

His grays were called Quaker Lady and Quaker Gent. Other than the fact that one was a mare and the other a gelding, you couldn't tell 'em part. Except from the driver seat, when their tails were up. Boy, could they trot. We passed so many other rigs on the way to Rutland, I lost count. They sure were a pair. And Mr. Tanner was as proud of that brace of grays as he was of Bob and Bib. He just cottoned to things in twos. I was about to ask him why he didn't keep a second Mrs. Tanner around somewhere, just as a matched pair to take out on Sunday. Or why he didn't just wed twins. But I remembered "manners" and owed up to silence.

"Never miss a chance," Papa had once said, "to keep your mouth shut." And the more I studied on it, the sounder it grew.

We got to Rutland the same time everybody else did. There couldn't of been nobody in Vermont who weren't there, and all dressed for Sabbath. It was some sight to see, even before we got to the Fair Grounds. It reminded me of the story I heard about a man from Learning who had gone all the way to the city of New York. When he got back, folks all asked him what the city was like. All he said was: "There was so much going on at the depot, I never got to the village."

I didn't know where the Rutland depot was. But it seemed to be about everywhere. And when we pulled up at the Fair Grounds, I was feared to blink for missing some of it.

The first place we headed for was where the stock was bedded down. Mrs. Tanner and I looked for what she called a "rest room." As it was still morning early, I wasn't of a mind to rest. But Mrs. Tanner sure was in a hurry for it. Bess was a big woman, and I never suspected she could cover so much distance in so short a time. We never did get to rest. All we did was find a pair of shanties, one marked LADIES and the other one GENTS. I knew right off it had something to do with where Mr. Tanner was going to put up his team. Even had their names on the door, and I thought that was real fancy. I sort of looked around for a shanty that said PINKY on the door, as they sure did things up fine in Rutland.

But it seemed like Bess Tanner was still in a big hurry to rest. She mumbled something about "riding that fast over those cussed bumps" and what it did to her insides. Must have been the reason she was tired. Just before she pushed me through the GENTS door, she whispered a word of warning about the place.

"Don't speak to a soul inside there, you hear? Places like that are full of perverts."

There wasn't much to do inside except take a leak, which I did. I looked around to see if I could spot me a pervert. As I was the only one in the place, there was no one to ask. I'd overheard Aunt Matty say "pervert" to Mama and Aunt Carrie, when they were talking. So I just figured that a pervert had something to do with grammar. Or maybe it was something like a cornet. But if'n there was a pervert in the place, they sure kept it hid. I sure hoped I'd see me one or two before we left Rutland, seeing as both Bess Tanner and Aunt Matty were so keen on them.

Mr. Tanner was outside, waiting for us. And the next thing we did was to go see Bob and Bib. The best part was that Pinky was close by, only one shed away. I jumped into her pen and put my arms around her neck and hugged her tight.

"Pinky," I said, "we're at Rutland. Ain't it grand?"

Right away quick we got Bob and Bib yoked and bowed. Bob was always left and Bib right. We went across an open show area, where some men were exercising some big horses with hairy hoofs, to find a photographer. We spent the better part of an hour getting our picture took. The man who owned the camera got up under a big black tent. His wife held a funny looking geegaw up in the air. It looked like some sort of snow shovel to me. But it was the first snow shovel I ever see explode. You never saw such a bang of light on a cloudy day in your life. I never saw the World War but it sure must of been like that. I almost jumped out of my boots. Bob and Bib didn't take kindly to it either. They backed into me, and started fighting the yoke. I tried to still 'em but I couldn't see. When the snow shovel went off, I was looking right at it . . . and it was the last thing I saw for quite a spell. It was a tribulation to me, too. Because we come to Rutland Fair to see a lot more than a damn fool snow shovel go off.

It come time to show the oxen. You should of seen 'em. Big as August first. Mr. Tanner nodded to a yoke of Herefords and said they'd weigh up about a ton each.

"Will Bob and Bib get that big?" I asked.

"Bigger. On account that Bob and Bib are Holstein, and they're the biggest and best."

I sure was proud to hear that. Even prouder when we went to the ox pull. When there was a pause in the contest, the man (who was talking through a big thing on his mouth that made his voice louder) called out Mr. Tanner's name.

"Exhibition only, and not for sale. From the town of Learning, a perfect yoke of matched yearlings by name of Bob and Bib, owned by Mr. Benjamin Franklin Tanner, and worked in the ring by Mr. Robert Peck."

That was my cue to take Bob and Bib around

the ring three times and then out. But I couldn't move. Until Mr. Tanner gave me a healthy prod in the backside with his goad and said, "Git!"

There I be. Me, at Rutland Fair, marching around a big sawdust ring with all the people clapping their hands and pointing at Bob and Bib. It made my heart pound so hard I felt it was going to pump out right there in that ring. I was wishing that Mama and Papa and Aunt Carrie could see. Pinky, too. It was sinful, but I wanted the whole town of Learning to see me just this once. If only Edward Thatcher could see. And Jacob Henry, and Becky Tate.

Parading my oxen around the ring and listening to the people clapping made me squint my eyes up tight. I could see all the folks I know, sitting there in those big circles of seats. "Manners," I said to myself, and walked real tall. It was just like I was somebody.

A man leaned over the fence and said to me, "What's their line, boy?"

"Out of Apron, Mr. Tanner's prize milker," I said. "The sire bull was his, too."

"Beowolf?"

"Yes, sir."

After three times round the ring, I touched Bib lightly on his right ear with my wand. The two little oxen made a smart left turn, and out we went through the gate. The people were still clapping and yelling. Some even followed us along, asking questions about Bob and Bib as we walked 'em back to their shed.

Somehow, Bess Tanner was not about in the crowd. I figured she probably was taking another rest. I'd given her up for gone, when I looked up and here she was coming on a dead run. I could just see the top of her head and her big floppy hat with all the flowers on it that weren't real.

Between her and us there was a passel of people, and they just seemed to melt out of the way for Mrs. Tanner. She was so short of breath when she got to us, she couldn't talk. She needed a rest for sure. I kind of hoped that maybe she'd finally spotted a pervert, and was just itching to tell folks.

"Quick," she said to me between her wheezes. "The 4-H Club men are judging the stock that the children raised up."

"Hogs?" said Mr. Tanner.

"No, they're looking the calves right now. But the hogs are next. I'll pen up the oxen. You take Rob with you, because I can't run another step in these shoes."

"Let's get Pinky," said Mr. Tanner, and we were off. Over in the next shed, most of the stock was gone. Pinky was almost the only pig there. We threw the bars open on her pen, and were just about to drive her out. That's when I noticed that she'd been rolling in something that wasn't very clean.

On her left shoulder and flank, she had a big dung stain. The rest of her was so clean (thanks to Mr. Tanner's stock man) that the dirty spot stuck out like a mean tongue. I went down on my knees and attacked the dirt with my hands and fingernails. It not only looked bad, but it stunk worse. The strong smell of its freshness made my eyes sting.

"Boy," said Ben Tanner, "that ain't no way to wash a pig."

"What'll wash her?"

"Same thing as washes a dirty pig and a dirty boy. Soap and water. Find soap. I'll fill a bucket and we're in business."

I must have turned Rutland upside down just trying to find some soap. I finally saw a bar of saddle soap in a tackroom, and made for it. But a man saw me and said, "Hey!"

"Soap," I said. "I'll buy your soap. My pig's dirty and the 4-H people are judging and we'll miss out. Here, all I got is ten cents. It's in this hanky and you can have it all."

I put the hanky (with Aunt Carrie's dime inside it) into his hand, grabbed the soap, and ran out the door. The man just couldn't say a word.

There went my ride on the merry-go-round. Into

a bar of soap. But I was too rushed to care. Mr. Tanner had a rag and in no time I got Pinky as clean as Christmas. Most of the water I managed to put on myself, and I was soaked through. And there was so much stink still on my hands, in spite of all the soap and water, that I figured I'd never would be able to eat a noon meal.

Mr. Tanner said that I took so long putting a scrub to Pinky that we'd never get there in time. But we did.

The kids were walking around an open ring, and each one had a pig. One boy had a real good-to-look-at Poland China, as white as Pinky but not as big. A girl who was taller than I was had a Spotted Poland, and a boy with red hair and lots of freckles had a fine looking Hampshire. It was coal black, with a white belt around it at the shoulder. Had it been a calf, it could of been a sister to Bob and Bib.

Some of the pigs were acting up a bit; not staying in line, and squealing all the time they was handled by the 4-H judges. The circle was just about whole when we got there, and Mr. Tanner almost threw me and Pinky into it just as another man closed up the gate.

My face was wet with the sweat of hurry. It feels worse, Papa always said, than the sweat of work. I didn't have a hanky to use, so as I stood there, I put my hand up to my brow. And right then I got such a whiff of pig manure I thought I'd pass out. Everything I ever ate went sour and wanted to come up my gullet. The judges were coming my way, but it just didn't matter. All the noise of Rutland Fair, and all the music and dust of the place just seemed to float off in a big whirly dream. I didn't need no ride on a merry-go-round, as all of Rutland was spinning about my head and taking me with it.

One of my eyes was closed shut. But the one that was part open got a quick look-see at a judge putting something on Pinky. Something blue. But when my whole entire world was green, I couldn't of cared. I just couldn't of cared if they'd put a pig sticker into both of us. The judge said something to me, and that's when I did it. I just leaned my head over, pointed my face at all the little square chips of sawdust, and threw up. Some of it even went on his shoe.

The merry-go-round went a whole lot faster, and I'd a fall off for certain. But some big strong hands reached out and caught me, or over I'd a gone.

"He's my charge," I heard Mr. Tanner say. "I'll take him."

Next thing I knew, we were all back at Pinky's pen. I was lying in fresh straw just outside it. Pinky was inside. Mr. Tanner was standing close by, and Mrs. Tanner was washing my face with a clean towel.

"How could you let him get so dirty?" was all she seemed to say to her husband. Mr. Tanner bent down and put his hand under my chin.

"Rob, how do you feel?"

"Hungry," I said.

"Look," he said, pointing at Pinky's neck. "Just look here."

It was a blue ribbon! And on it, in gold letters, it said:

FIRST PRIZE FOR BEST-BEHAVED PIG

"It's just about noon," he said. "Let's all put on the feed bag. What say, Bessie?"

Bess Tanner just sighed. "Start without me. I don't want to put anything on right now. I just want to take off this cussed corset."

Chapter

II

"Pinky won a blue ribbon, Papa."

That was the first thing I said when Ben Tanner shook me awake that night to tell me I was home. I must of slept all the way, because I didn't recall much of the trip back. Soon as it got dark I just went to sleep, sitting there between Mr. and Mrs. Tanner and holding on tight to the blue ribbon.

"Pinky won a blue ribbon. It's for the best-behaved pig," I said.

"And," said Mr. Tanner, "he ought to have a second one for best-behaved boy. He worked my oxen like he was born with a wand in his hand."

"How were his manners?" asked Papa.

"Thank you, Mr. Tanner," I said quickly. "And thank you, Mrs. Tanner. I had a very good time."

"Bless you, Rob," she said.

"The stock'll be here soon as the Fair closes," Mr. Tanner said.

"I'll send the boy for his pig," Papa said, "and we're beholding to both you folks, Brother Tanner."

"We to you, Haven. I got offered five hundred for my yearling oxen. Five hundred dollars, and not even half growed. Thanks to your boy who helped born 'em, and work 'em at the Fair. But I won't sell them two."

"I'm glad he did you proud," Papa said.

Ben Tanner turned his grays and off they went, Bess holding her hat on with the flat of her hand. I just stood there and watched them go up road into the dark, and until I could no longer hear their rig.

"Good neighbors," I said.

"The best a man could have," said Papa. "Benjamin Tanner will stand without hitching."

Mama came running out of the house and toward the barn, holding out her hands. I ran to her and hugged her clean and warm and hard as I could. Aunt Carrie was there, too. I wanted to tell her (as I hugged her) as to how I spent the ten cents that she gave me, but I thought better of it. Ten cents for a used piece of saddle soap was a dear price.

"Mama," I said, "looky here. Look at Pinky's blue ribbon! She won it."

"Of course she won it," Mama said. "She's the prettiest pig in Learning."

"First prize," I said. I remembered in a faint sort

of way that the other pigs that the kids had raised all had blue ribbons, too. But no matter. I was sure that only Pinky had won first prize.

"She'll be home in a few days," I said.

"I can't wait," said Papa, and Mama smiled.

"Into the house with you," Mama said. "It's way past your bedtime and you'll never get up for chores." That sort of stopped me.

"Papa? You did all my chores today."

"Sure did. And butchered hogs besides."

"Thank you, Papa. I'm beholding."

"I accept your debt," Papa said, "and come 'morrow, you'll work double."

"That's meet and right," I said. "I already owe you for the sorghum."

"Three bags full," said Papa. "I expect payment after your pig has a first litter."

Mama said, "You men folk don't know when it's time for bed. How about some pie, Rob?"

"Please," I said.

We all sat around the lammis table in the kitchen, eating blackberry pie, and hearing me talk about Rutland Fair. I told all I could tell and made up the rest, and never left out a word about the two main events: the showing of Bob and Bib, and the blue ribbon for Pinky.

I never let on that I got a touch of the vapors and

lost all my breakfast on the judge's shoe. A tale like that would only distress Mama and Aunt Carrie, so why tell people what they don't cotton to hear? Besides, they was enough good things to jaw on. Like when the whole state of Vermont watched me work the oxen in the show ring, and how the man shouted my name. I stood up and gave a real close copy of just how he done it. Even marched around the kitchen in a circle. Three times, just like at Rutland.

"Rutland," said Papa. "I never went there, boy or man. And here *you* go, all that way by your lonesome with the neighbors."

"It's not so big," I said. "What sets you back is the noise. It was as noisy at night as it was in the morning. And during Fair week, I guess it's like a big brass band that can't stop playing. Goes all the while."

"Just like a mouth I know," said Papa, "that's got blackberry all over it."

We all got a good laugh on that, before I went over to the sink pump and washed off. It sure was good to be home, and it was hard to believe that I was gone less than a day. It felt like I'd been to a star.

I'd a talked on about Rutland for the whole night through, but Mama chased me upstairs to bed. Once I was under the covers, she came into my room and kissed me goodnight. I was just about near asleep by the time she tiptoed out and shut the door.

"How's the traveler?" I heard Papa ask.

"Back," Mama said. "Back from a dream."

During the night, there was noise outside in the hen coop. I heard the hens cackle and scold. I saw a lit lantern in the upstairs hall, and then all was quiet. I tried my holy best to wake up, but I just couldn't.

Right after I shut my eyes it was chore time. Daisy had to be milked and watered and fed. Solomon the same. Except only a fool would put a pail under him. I was pouring the milk for separating (to get the cream off) when I saw Papa leaving the hen coop with a dead hen.

"Weasel," Papa said. "And hardly no mark on her."

"Chicken for supper, Papa?"

"Yup. Say, you want to see something?"

"Sure."

Papa took me into the tackroom. Hanging on a peg was a burlap sack that moved around a bit. Quite a bit, the closer we got.

"What you got, Papa?"

"What I got is that weasel. First one I ever could corner and sack. He's really got a mouthful of mean teeth."

"Can I look?"

"Later. When I reason out what to do with him. He's caused me too much grief to kill without a ceremony."

"You aim to let that weasel go free?"

"Not likely."

"Papa, I was at Mrs. Bascom's last week."

"So?"

"You know her hired man, Ira Long?"

"Heard his name."

"Well, he's got a bitch terrier. I seen her when I went to thank Mrs. Bascom for asking the Tanners to take me to Rutland."

"Full growed?"

"I'd say so, Papa. But real young."

"After we breakfast, boy, you run down there and tell Brother Long that we got a weasel to try his dog on. And he's welcome to it."

"Sure will. I never see a dog get weaseled."

An hour later, a horse and rig pulled into our lane. On it was Ira Long and me and his dog, Hussy. She was a sweet little dog, and all the way home, as I was holding her, I wondered how well she'd fair against a weasel.

Papa was there to meet us, and he gave Ira his hand.

"Haven Peck," he said. "We're glad you could pay us call, Brother."

"Ira Long. I already know your son."

"Most folks do." Both the men laughed. I don't know why but I laughed, too.

"He's a good 'un," said Ira.

Papa looked at the small gray-and-white terrier that I was still holding in my arms. "You tried that bitch on weasel yet?"

"No. But I hear you got one."

"A big one," Papa said. "Mean as sin."

"Papa," I said, "why do folks weasel a dog? Is it for the sport of it?"

"No," Papa said, "there's earthy reason. 'Cause once you weasel that dog, that dog'll hate weasels until her last breath. She'll always know when there's one around and she'll track it to its hole, dig it out, and tear it up. A man who keeps a hen house got to have a good weasel dog."

"That's the truth of it," Ira said. "Every weasel in the county will keep wide of my little Hussy."

When the three of us walked into the tackroom I was still carrying Hussy. Soon as we got there, that burlap jumped around like it was loco. And I could feel Ira's little terrier shaking in my arms. Just like she knew what was going to happen, and what she'd got to do to stay alive. She was whining, too. Just loud enough to hear.

"I got an idea she'll make a good weasel dog," Ira said.

"We'll see," said Papa.

He picked the sack off its peg. Inside, the weasel was hissing and spitting. He couldn't see a dog, and she couldn't see him. But they knew. They sure knew of each other.

"I'll get a barrel," I said. Handing the bitch to Ira, I ran up to the cellar where there was a good size apple barrel that was empty and waiting for this year's orchard. It had a wooden lid on it which made it perfect for what we wanted it for. I set the barrel on its side. Holding the lid under one arm, I rolled the barrel down to where the men were waiting. Ira was holding his terrier, and Papa had the neck of the burlap bag tight in his hand. I stood the barrel up on its end, mouth open, and holding the lid ready.

"In you go, Hussy," Ira said, placing his little bitch inside the barrel. "You give him what for."

She sure was shaking, that dog. It made the whole barrel sort of tremble. Papa came forward with the sack.

"Is your lid ready?" he said to me.

"All set."

"Soon's I drop him from the sack, you lid that barrel and keep it lidded, hear?"

"Yes, Papa."

Without more ado, Papa just emptied the sack. He poured the weasel right down inside the barrel on top of the dog. I slammed the lid into place. I could hardly hold it on, and Ira come over to keep the barrel upright. Papa, too.

We heard a lot of scratching and chasing and biting inside the dark of that barrel. The dog was bigger, but the weasel sure had the darkness on his side. To be honest, I thought a fight between a dog and a weasel was going to be a real excitement. But I hated every second of it. The whole thing seemed senseless to me and I was mad at myself for standing there to hold down the barrel lid. I even felt the shame of being a part of it. From the look on Papa's face I could see that maybe he wasn't enjoying it so much either.

At last all the noise stopped. There wasn't a sound. Papa nodded to me, and I slipped the lid a crack, just enough to let some light in so we could look down inside. Then we heard the dog cry. It was a whine that I will always remember, the kind of sound that you hear but never want to hear again.

Ira pulled the lid of the barrel away and looked inside. The weasel was dead. Torn apart into small pieces of fur, bones, and bloody meat. There was blood all over the inside of that barrel, from top to bottom. The dog was alive, but not much more. One of her ears was about tore off and she was wet with blood. She just danced her little feet, splattering the pool of blood in the bottom of the barrel. And making that sound in her throat that almost begged someone to end her misery.

Ira reached down to lift her out of the barrel. As he picked her up, her teeth bared and she ripped open his hand. He gave out a yell and dropped her on the ground. One of her front paws was chewed up so bad, it wasn't even a paw anymore. All of the bones in that foot must have been split to pieces. It was nothing but a raw stump.

"Kill her," I said.

"What?" said Ira, his hand bleeding into the cuff of his shirt.

"She's dying," I said. "And if you got any mercy at all in you, Ira Long, you'll do her in. Right now. She killed the weasel. Isn't that what you wanted to have her do, with all its sport? She's crazy with hurt. And if you don't kill her, I will."

"Mind your tongue, boy. You're talking to your elders," said Ira.

"The boy's right," Papa said. "I'll get a gun."

Until Papa come back with the rifle, little Hussy just lay on the ground and whimpered. Papa put a bullet in her, and her whole body jerked to a quivering stillness. Nobody said a word. The three of us just stood there, looking down into the dust at what once was a friendly little pet.

"I swear," Papa said. "I swear by the Book of Shaker and all that's holy, I will never again weasel a dog. Even if I lose every chicken I own."

I got a spade out of the tool room, and dug a small hole, and buried her under the timothy grass, near an apple tree. I even got down on my knees and said her a prayer.

"Hussy," I said, "you got more spunk in you than a lot of us menfolk got brains."

Chapter

12

Pinky came home.

I had her blue ribbon pinned up on the wall over my bed, and took it out to show it to her. She sniffed at it and that was about all.

"You can be a right proud pig, Pinky," I said, scratching her back. "You're the best-behaved pig in the whole state of Vermont."

She just snorted to that, and I was glad she wasn't getting too filled with herself. A swell-headed pig would be hard to live with. I ran into the house and put the blue ribbon back on its pin over my bed. When I got back outside, Papa was home from butchering. His clothes were a real mess.

"Papa," I said, "after a whole day at rendering pork, don't you start to hate your clothes?"

"Like I could burn 'em and bury 'em."

"But you wear a leather apron when you kill pork. How come you still get so dirty?"

"Dying is dirty business. Like getting born."

"I never thought of it that way. But I'm sure glad that nobody'll kill Pinky. She's going to be a brood sow, isn't she Papa?"

He didn't answer. He just walked over to the fence and looked at my pig. Swinging his leg over the rails, he knelt down beside her and run his hand along her back. He looked at her rump real close, smelled her, and felt her backside with his hand.

"What's wrong, Papa? Is Pinky ailing?"

"No, not ailing. Just slow. She should of had her first heat by now. Weeks ago. We could a bred her to boar at the third. Maybe she's barren."

"Barren? You mean . . . "

"I don't know for sure, boy. Just maybe she's barren."

"Like Aunt Matty?"

"Yes. But that's not to talk of. You'd hurt Matty if'n you said barren to her face. The hurt's inside her. No need to fester it."

"And you think Pinky's barren? Tell me true, Papa."

"Yes, boy. I think she be."

"No," I said. "No! No!"

My fists were doubled and I hit the top rail of the fence, harder and harder. Until my hands started to hurt.

"Rob, that won't change nothing. You got to face what is."

He climbed over the fence and walked to the barn, his tall lean body moving as if it knew more work would be done that day, tired or no.

"Rob!" Mama called to me from the kitchen door, and I left Pinky and ran up the hill to where she was standing, drying her hands on her apron.

"Go get a squirrel," she said, smiling.

Inside the house, I took the .22 rifle off the lintel over the fireplace, dropped some cartridges in my pocket, and went back outside. I should of been happy, going squirrel hunting, but I just wasn't.

There was a stand of hickory trees up on the west end of the ridge, on the yonder side of the spar mine. Now that it was autumn, the walnuts would be ripe and eaten. As I climbed up the ridge, I started searching the trees for a gray, a big fat one with a full paunch.

High in a nearby pin oak, there was a round brown ball of dead leaves and twigs. There was no movement near it, but I stood soldier still and waited. My eyes rolled into the tops of the other trees, but saw nothing. There just wasn't a gray squirrel to be had. I walked up and into the trees, and sat on a stump. Looking down across the valley, it was yellow with golden rod. Like somebody broke eggs all over the hillside.

Then I heard him! He was just over my head, sitting flat on a branch, twitching his long gray brush of a tail. And making that scolding squirrel chip-chip-chip-chip-chip sort of a sound. Sassy as salt. A round was already in the chamber. Raising the gun, I put the black bead of the front sight deep in the V-notch of the rear sight. The bead was just behind his ear when I squeezed the trigger.

It was like he was yanked off the limb by a rope. He fell kicking into a mess of leaves and brush, and when I got to him he was still twisting. Holding his back legs, I swung his body against the trunk of a sweet gum tree. His spine cracked, and he was dead.

Back on the kitchen stoop, I took a knife and cut open his belly. I was right careful not to cut the paunch. Removing the warm wet sack, I brought it into the kitchen, and washed it under the sink pump. Mama had a clean white linen hanky ready. I lanced the paunch and we emptied all the chewed-up nutmeats on it, spreading them out so they'd dry. Mama put the hanky up in the warming oven above the stove.

I couldn't see the chocolate cake, but it had to be around somewheres. If there was no cake, Mama wouldn't of wanted a gray. Outside, I cut up the rest of the squirrel and threw it to the chickens. They fought over the big hunks, and the larger hens bulled the weaker ones away. The scrawny ones got nothing. I was thinking about that, when Papa come up behind me. We watched the matron hens eat, while the runts just watched.

"It isn't fair, is it, Papa?"

"Rob, it ain't a fair world."

"How are the apples doing? You think it's time we picked?"

"Two more days," Papa said. "They ain't good this year, and we can't let any drop. The spanner worms were so heavy last June, it ate up lots of the buds."

"We smoked, Papa."

"That we did. But maybe the mix was wrong. Tell me again, boy, what you did."

"Just like you said, Pa. It was last May when I scraped all the black ash off the inside of the fireplace and the cookstove. I mixed in the quicklime, and split it up so's I could put a pile of it under every apple tree in the orchard."

"How many?"

"Eighteen. We lost one to winter."

"You add the water to the mix like I told you?"

"Yes, Papa. I threw about a cup on each pile and the mix hissed up real good. It really smoked up proper."

"Was it windy?"

"Come to think, it was. Some of the vapors got blowed away."

"Boy, you got to put ash and lime always windward to the tree. Test the breeze for each tree. Currents are strange in an orchard."

"I did it wrong. That's why the spanners were so numbered."

"You'll do right next spring, Rob. Just take time with things. One chore done good beats two done ragged."

"Yes, sir."

"You can always look to how a farm is tended and know the farmer. Ever see Brother Tanner's place?"

"Sure. Lots of times."

"I don't mean just see it. I mean to study it. His fence is straight and white as virtue. All the critters are clean. Mark how he cuts his hay. Ain't no truer windrow in all of Learning."

"He's a good farmer," I said.

"He'll walk to his barn at six and six. You could set a clock at the first chime of milk that hits the pail."

"Is he a better farmer than you, Papa?"

"Yes. He bests me at it. He wouldn't say to my face. But he knows and I know, and there's not a use in wording it."

"I don't want to grow up to be like Mr. Tanner. I want to be like you, Papa."

"I wouldn't wish that on a dead cat."

"I do, Papa. And I will. I'll be just like you."

"No, boy, you won't. You have your schooling. You'll read and write and cipher. And when you spray that orchard, you'll use the new things."

"Chemicals?"

"True. And you'll have more than farming to do. You won't have to leave your land to kill another man's hogs, and then ask for the grind meat with your hat in your hand."

"But you're a good butcher, Papa. Even Mr. Tanner said you were the best in the county."

"He say that?"

"Honest, Papa. He said he could look at half a pork and tell it was you that boiled and scraped it. He said you even had your own trade mark. When you kill pork and twain it, head to rump, you always do what no other man does. You even divide the tail, and half it right to the end. He said this on the way to Rutland."

"I'm sure glad to be famed for something."

"Supper's on!" Mama called out from the kitchen. "You two menfolk intend to stand all evening and preach to the hens?"

"With only one rooster," Papa yelled up to her, "I doubt they *need* much preaching."

Mama laughed, and went inside. We followed, after washing up proper at the pump. Papa put his hand on my shoulder as we walked up to the house.

"Try an' try," he said, "but when it comes day's end, I can't wash the pig off me. And your mother never complains. Not once, in all these years, has she ever said that I smell strong. I said once to her that I was sorry."

"What did Mama say?"

"She said I smelled of honest work, and that there was no sorry to be said or heard."

We had a good supper, with hot biscuit and honey. And after, we had chocolate cake. The nutmeats that we'd took out of the squirrel were dry. Aunt Carrie took 'em out the warming oven and sprinkled them on top of the cake. Like little white stars in a big brown heaven. And I got cut a slice of that cake that even Solomon couldn't of moved.

Later, after chores and dishes were done, Mama and Aunt Carrie were talking in the kitchen. Papa and I sat in the parlor near the fireplace. We'd had a fire going earlier, but now it was dying down. Ready for bed, like people. Cold weather was coming, and coming for sure. But it felt good to have a fire in the hearth, and it was sure a grand thing to look at while you talked.

Papa said once that wood heats you three times. When you cut it, haul it, and burn it.

"Winter's coming, Papa."

"True enough."

"I think I may need a new winter coat."

"Better speak to your mother to start stitching."

"I want a store coat. I *need* one."

"So do I. But one thing to learn, Rob, is this. *Need* is a weak word. Has nothing to do with what people get. Ain't what you need that matters. It's what you do. And your mother'll do you a coat."

"Just once," I said. "Just one time I'd hanker for a store-bought coat. A red and black buffalo plaid checkerboard coat, just like Jacob Henry's. Just once I'd like to walk in the General Store with money in my pocket and touch all them coats. Every one. Touch 'em all and smell all the *new* that's in 'em. Like new boots."

"That would be fine. Real fine," Papa said.

"Jacob Henry said that in one store in Learning they let you wear all the coats you want before you buy one. And you can put on any coat you want and walk around the store in it, even if you don't buy it. But you know what I'd do. I'd buy a red and black one, like Jacob Henry's. It would be my coat forever, and I'd never wear it out."

"Reckon you'd outgrow it before you outwear it."

"Probably would. But I sure do want a coat like that. Why do we have to be Plain People? Why do we, Papa?"

"Because we are."

"I guess I'll never have a coat like that. Can I?"

"You can. When you earn one. You'll be a man one day. One day soon."

"Someday," I said.

"It can't be someday, Rob. It's got to be now. This winter. Your sisters are gone, all four are wedded and bedded. Your two brothers are dead. Born dead and grounded in our orchard. So it's got to be you, Rob."

"Why are you saying this, Papa?"

"Because, son. Because this is my last winter. I got an affection, I know I do."

"You seen Doc Knapp?"

"No need. All things end, and so it goes."

"No, Papa. Don't say that."

"Listen, Rob. Listen, boy. I tell you true. You got to face up to it. You can't be a boy about it."

"Papa, Papa . . . "

"You are not to say this to your mother, or to Carrie. But from now on, you got to listen how to run this farm. We got five years to go on it, and the land is ours. Lock and stock. Five years to pay off. And you'll be through school by then."

"I'll quit school and work the farm."

"No you won't. You stay and get schooled. Get all the teaching you can hold."

I got up from the chair I was in so as I could be near him. I touched the sleeve of his shirt and felt his whole body stiffen. He looked away as he spoke.

"It's got to be you, Rob. Your mother and Carrie can't do it alone. Come spring, you aren't the boy of the place. You're the man. A man of thirteen. But no less a man. And whatever has to be done on this land, it's got to be did by you, Rob. Because there'll be nobody else, boy. Just you."

"Papa, no."

"It can't be no longer your mother and Carrie taking care of you. Soon you got to care for them. They're old, too. Years of work's done that. Your ma's not young anymore, and Carrie is near seventy."

"Seventy?"

"Yes, boy. So to short the story, I could be wrong. But I feel like it's over for me soon. Animals know when. And I reckon I'm more beast than man."

I didn't believe it, and I couldn't say anything. I just hoped he'd reach out and touch me or kiss me or something. But he just got up from his chair, wrapped a hot rock from the fireplace in a sack for his bed, and went upstairs. Mama and Aunt Carrie had left the kitchen and gone up, too. The parlor was still and dark.

I sat watching the red cinders turn gray. I stayed there until the fire died. So it would not have to die alone.

Chapter

13

October came, with colors as pretty as laundry on a line. Then it was November, and on dark mornings on the way to the barn to milk Daisy, I thought the air would snap my lungs.

For weeks, Papa had looked at Pinky every day. He even said I should feed her some new food, and to mix some meat scraps into her mash. Enough to turn her wild and make her heat. But there was no estrus. No sign of Pinky coming to age. I saw Mr. Tanner up on the ridge with his Purdy, gunning for grouse. And so I told him about my pig, and that there was no estrus. No heat. I asked him if he thought Pinky was barren. He said he'd stop over next morning.

He did. I was hardly through chores when I heard the rattle of an oxcart coming down the road. It was Bob and Bib, and were they ever growed! Behind him as he sat, the wagon sides were slatted up and I couldn't see what was inside. As he turned in, I ran out to meet him.

"Morning, Brother," I said.

"Morning, Robert. Fine day."

I looked between the cart slats and there he was, the finest boar in the county. Big and mean and all male. No one could of ever eat him. His ham would of been strong as tree bark, and full of tack.

"Where's your gilt?" Mr. Tanner asked.

"Around back," I said, pointing to where we kept Pinky.

"Your pa home?"

"No," I said. "He left early. November is a busy time for his work."

"No matter," said Ben Tanner. "The reason why of it is this. Perhaps your pig is barren, perhaps no. Sometimes a girl just has to be coaxed and courted. You and I can't get Pinky to heat, because to her eyes we're not that handsome. But wait until she gets a smell of Samson. He can smell heat when we can't. And if he does, she'll change her tune."

We backed the oxcart to the small box pen, and put a ramp up for Samson. Removing the slats with Mr. Tanner, I got a look at that boar for the first time. He must have weighed four or even five hundred, and he was one big Poland. Mr. Tanner gave him a prod and he left the cart walking down the ramp like a king. In his nose, the big brass ring caught the sun and it shined real bright.

"All my sows are farrowed, so he'll be more than happy to help. He's been in a pen by his lonesome longer than a week. And he's due."

I went around back and called Pinky. But she wouldn't come, and she was too darn big to push, so I had to take a small switch to her. I swatted her good and proper all the way to the box pen, and in she went to mix with Samson. As she walked through the gate, Ben slapped a handful of lard on her rump. Under her tail.

Pinky was large. But next to him, she looked only about half growed. She just looked at him, her nose close to the ground like it always was, trying to get a smell that would tell her what he was. Her rump had been dry as dust, but that didn't mean that it couldn't heat.

Samson grunted. He walked to her and pushed her with his nose. She let him push her like that once more, then she backed away from him. He walked to her and by her, rubbing his shoulder against hers. He tried to smell her rump, but she bolted, kicking away at him with her hind feet. Several times he tried to get a good whiff of her, but she wasn't holding still for it. Turning on him she got her teeth onto his ear and tore its edge before Mr. Tanner could whack her a sharp blow with his stick.

"All part of courting," said he. "Samson just got his face slapped. That's all."

The two hogs just stood there looking at each other, not doing anything. That's when Ben Tanner lit up his pipe.

"Your father," he said. "How's his health?"

He asked the question real easy, like it didn't matter none. But I knew it did. Ben Tanner looked at me when I didn't say up, and he wanted an answer.

"Fine," I said. "Papa's so sturdy, he never missed a day slaughtering his entire life."

I had to look away when I said it, and had no idea what I could of said next. As I was trying to think of something, Miss Sarah came out of the barn. Her three kittens were with her, but now they too were growed up almost as mighty as Miss Sarah herself.

"Those are Miss Sarah's kittens," I said. "All growed."

"That old barn cat of mine, the big buff I call Caleb. If he ain't the tom that serviced that litter I'll ride Samson all the way home."

Looking at Samson, I figured there wasn't a man

living or dead who could straddle him. He was one mean looking boar. Had a mean mouth, even though Ben Tanner probably tried to cut back each tusk with pliers or wire cutters. It was no picnic, I would wager, being a dentist to Samson.

"Now that Caleb come to trespass on Miss Sarah," I said, "it sure would be fitting if Samson would breed Pinky."

"Sure would. But mind, son. If he does, I expect a stud fee."

"Stud fee?"

"Fifty dollars," said Mr. Tanner, smiling. "Or two picks of the litter. You're to choose."

"You can have two of her brood," I said.

"Done."

Now it was no longer a friendly visit; now it was real business, and Samson seemed to guess what we all expected of him. Butting hard into Pinky's front shoulder with his snout, he half turned her about. Quick as silver, he jumped to her rear, pinning her up against the fence. Up on his back legs, he came down hard upon her, his forelegs up on her shoulders. His privates were alert and ready to breed her, and as she tried to move out from under him, he moved with her. His back legs strained forward to capture her, and his entire back and body was thrusting again and again. Pinky was squealing from his weight and the hurt of his forcing himself to her.

As I watched, I hated Samson. I hated him for being so big and mean and heavy. Even when her front legs buckled from all the weight of him being on her, he never eased up. But he was a real boar and a prize boar and there was no stopping him.

"You wait," said Ben Tanner. "There ain't a sow in Vermont that'll deny Samson. He's all boar."

Samson was all boar, it proved true. He was bigger and stronger and ten times meaner than Pinky. So he had his way with her. All the time he was breeding into her, she squealed like her throat had been cut. Every breath. She just squealed like crying, and wouldn't stop. Not even after Samson had enough of her and got down off her, did she stop her whining. Not even then.

Her rump was bruised and there was blood running down her hind leg. She was shaking like she couldn't stand, her whole body quivering. I started to swing a leg over the fence so I could pat her a bit and clean her up. But I felt Ben Tanner's strong hand on my shoulder, pulling me back.

"You crazy, boy? You go into that pen now and go near her, and that boar will have you for breakfast. Where's your sense?"

"I guess I don't have any," I said.

"Time you got some. How old be you, Rob?"

"Twelve, sir. I'll be thirteen, come February."

"Good. Twelve's a boy, thirteen a man. Now just take Pinky there. She weren't nought but a maiden before this morning. Just a little girl, she was. A big little girl. But from this time on, she's a sow. She knows a thing or two. And next time, she'll welcome the big boy. Even ram herself through barbwire to be with him and get bred by him. Understand?"

"Yes, sir. I think so."

"Your pa is slaughtering today, is he?"

"Yes."

"Hard work. He ought to take it easy one of these days, now he's got you to man the place."

"Papa works all the time. He don't never rest. And worse than that, he works inside himself. I can see it on his face. Like he's been trying all his life to catch up to something. But whatever it is, it's always ahead of him, and he can't reach it."

"You reason all that out by your lonesome?"

"Yes, sir."

"You're a keen lad, for a Shaker boy. How are your lessons?"

"I get A in everything. Almost."

"Everything?"

"Everything except English. I don't never get an A in that, and darned if I know why."

"Maybe the teacher doesn't like you."

"The teacher is Miss Malcolm. She likes me fine. But I still don't get no A in English."

"Strange."

"She says I have potential. It means that someday I could do a lot. Miss Malcolm says that I could be more than a farmer."

"More than a farmer?!" Ben Tanner looked a bit red. "What better can a man be? There's no higher calling than animal husbandry, and making things live and grow. We farmers are stewards. Our lot is to tend all of God's good living things, and I say there's nothing finer."

"That's what Papa says. In just five years, we'll own this farm. All of it."

"Glad to hear it. You Pecks are good neighbors."

I laughed.

"What's so funny?"

"That's what Papa and I always say about you folks. You're good neighbors."

"I watched all your sisters grow up. Pretty girls, they were. Prim and proper in every way, and a real credit to your folks."

"Thank you, Mr. Tanner."

"I was sad to hear when your two brothers were taken. Bess was, too. She spent time with your ma because of it. But now it's you, Robert. And you've got a start. Pinky is going to make you a fine brood sow. She'll farrow at least ten pigs, spring and fall—if you breed her fresh again just three days after she weans. That's twenty pigs a year. In five years, that's a hundred hogs."

"Gee! A hundred hogs."

"It's not the number alone, boy. Pinky ain't just another pig. She comes from a stout meaty line. So does Samson. The sow that bore him would often bear twelve instead of ten. Two extra. That's dollars, boy. Dollars you can pay off this farm with. Good solid Yankee dollars that you can bank."

All this talk of hogs and dollars and meat and banks was rolling around inside my head with no direction. It didn't quite sound Christian to me, but then I suppose that everyone in the world didn't all live strict by the Book of Shaker.

"But we're Plain People, sir. It may not be right to want for so much."

"Nonsense, boy. Bess and I are fearing Christians, same as you."

"But you aren't a Shaker. Are you?"

"No. I'm a Baptist! Wash feet and hard shell Baptist. Born one, and I hope to die one. But not yet. I'm a Baptist, and so's Bess."

I almost busted out laughing. There they were, the three people who probably loved me more than anyone in the whole world (besides Papa, Mama, and Aunt Carrie)—Mr. and Mrs. Tanner, and Aunt Matty. And all of them were good shouting Baptists. It just goes to show how wrong I could feel about some things.

And how foolish.

Chapter

14

The apple crop was bad.

The weather had turned colder, and we were lucky to get a few Baldwins and Jonathans barreled for wintering in the cellar. Papa had been right. The crop was lean. The apples that we did harvest were not large, and many had worm holes. The one tree that had died was our greening tree, one that produced smaller apples that were green and very tart. Pie apples. But this winter they'd be no pies.

Twice, Papa had seen a buck and several doe upon the ridge. But each time he got the shotgun and slug-shells ready, the deer were gone. Jacob Henry's father got a buck. So did Ira Long. One of the men who farmed for Ben Tanner got a doe. But Papa didn't have a deer rifle; only a shotgun with ball loads. He had to get close for a shot.

He still-hunted early almost every morning, hoping to get a buck deer before it was time to go to work. No luck. Once he even sat for four hours in a cold rain, waiting, He coughed after that; a deep rattling cough that made him hang on to things. But the worst thing was when his lungs got so bad he stopped sleeping with Mama. He slept in the barn. It was warmer there, with Daisy and Solomon both inclosed in a cozy area.

The first snow came. It wasn't very heavy; and when the next day's sun broke through, it all melted away. But more would follow.

Pinky did not have a litter of pigs. She was bred and she was barren. And she ate too much to keep as a pet. Samson had mounted her twice, and there was no litter. Nothing. And little estrus. She never really come to full heat, not even once.

It all ended one early morning on a dark December day. It was Saturday and there was no school. After chores, Papa and I came in for breakfast. I tried to down a big bowl of hot steaming oatmeal, but it tasted like soap. And the fresh warm milk from Daisy's pail was flat. I couldn't swallow it. Papa just sat at the kitchen table, fingering a pipe that he couldn't smoke and looking at a breakfast he couldn't eat. He finally got up from the table to look through the window. Outside, the dark of the moon was just softening into firstlight. When he turned round to me, his face was sober.

"Rob, let's get it done."

I didn't ask what. I just knew. And so did Mama and Aunt Carrie, because as Papa and I were getting our coats on to go outside, they both came over and pretended to help bundle me up.

There had been a light inch of snow the night before. Just enough to cover the ground the way Mama would flour her cake board. I followed Papa out to where we kept the tools, and I stood there watching as he sharpened the knives on the wheel. The sticking knife was short and blunt, with a curved blade. The edge he put to it was extra sharp. He pulled on some heavy rubber boots in the barn, and tied a sheath of leather around his middle, for an apron. We were ready.

Toting some of the tools and a spine saw, I followed him out of the shed and around to the south side of the barn, to where old Solomon and the capstan had pulled the corn cratch—Pinky's house. Inside it she was lying all curled up warm in the clean straw. It was a soft warm smell.

"Come on, Pinky," I tried to say in a cheerful way. "It's morning." But my throat seemed to catch and the words just wouldn't come out. I nudged her with my foot. But finally had to take a switch and make her get to her feet. She came to me, nuzzle pointed into my leg. Her curly tail was moving about like it was glad the day had started. People say pigs don't feel. And that they don't wag their tails. All I know is that Pinky sure knew who I was and her tail did too.

While Papa lit a fire to boil the water, I pushed her out of the crib and into a box pen, the same one that she'd been in when bred to Samson. She balked at the gate, and I had to hit her hard with the stick a few times to move her forward. It probably hurt her, but what did it matter now.

Following her into the box pen, we closed the gate by sliding the bars across. I got down on my knees in the snow and put my arms around her big white neck, smelling her good solid smell.

Pinky, I said to myself, try and understand. If there was any other way. If only Papa had got a deer this fall. Or if I was old enough to earn money. If only . . .

"Help me, boy," said Papa. "It's time."

He put his tools on the ground, keeping only a three-foot crowbar. Neither one of us wore gloves, and I knew how cold that crowbar felt. I'd carried it, and it was colder than death.

"Back away," he said.

"Papa," I said, "I don't think I can."

"That ain't the issue, Rob. We have to."

Standing up, I moved away from Pinky as Papa went to her head. She just stood there in the fresh snow, looking at my feet. I saw Papa get a grip on the crowbar, and raise it high over his head. It was then I closed my eyes, and my mouth opened like I wanted to scream for her. I waited. I waited to hear the noise that I finally heard.

It was a strong crushing noise that you only hear when an iron stunner bashes in a pig's skull. I hated Papa that moment. I hated him for killing her, and hated him for every pig he ever killed in his lifetime . . . for hundreds and hundreds of butchered hogs.

"Hurry," he said.

I opened my eyes and went to her. She was down in the snow. Moving, breathing, but down. I helped roll her over on her back, standing astride her and holding her two forelegs straight up in the air. With his left hand Papa pushed her chin down so that the top of her snout touched the ground. His right hand held the blunt knife with the curved blade. He stuck her throat deep and way back, moving the knife back through the neck toward himself, cutting the main neck artery. Her blood gushed bubbled out in heaving floods. Some of it went on my boots. I wanted to run, and cry and scream. But I just stood there, helping to hold her kicking.

It was all so quiet, like Christmas morning. As Papa continued to draw the pork, I held the feet firm and up. The blood was still pumping out of her, and the ground beneath our feet was spotted with hot pig blood steaming on the cold snow.

Between my ankles I could feel her body quiver in death. I had to look away. So as Papa worked on her, I held fast, staring at the old corn cratch that had once been Pinky's home.

Papa worked quiet and quick. The guts got drawed out and were there on the cold ground in a hot misty mass. Then we each put a hook in the jaws and dragged the bloody body into boiling water. It was boiled, scraped free of all hair and scurf, and sawed in half.

Papa was breathing the way no man or beast should breathe. I had never seen any man work as fast. I knew his hands must of been just about froze off; but he kept working, with no gloves. At last he stopped, pushing me away from the pork and turning me around so as my back was to it. He stood close by, facing me, and his whole body was steaming wet with work. I couldn't help it. I started thinking about Pinky. My sweet big clean white Pinky who followed me all over. She was the only thing I ever really owned. The only thing I could point to and say . . . *mine*. But now there was no Pinky. Just a sopping wet lake of red slush. So I cried.

"Oh, Papa. My heart's broke."

"So is mine," said Papa. "But I'm thankful you're a man."

I just broke down, and Papa let me cry it all out. I just sobbed and sobbed with my head up toward the sky and my eyes closed, hoping God would hear it.

"That's what being a man is all about, boy. It's just doing what's got to be done."

I felt his big hand touch my face, and it wasn't the hand that killed hogs. It was almost as sweet as Mama's. His hand was rough and cold, and as I opened my eyes to look at it, I could see that his knuckles were dripping with pig blood. It was the hand that just butchered Pinky. He did it. Because he had to. Hated to and had to. And he knew that he'd never have to say to me that he was sorry. His hand against my face, trying to wipe away my tears, said it all. His cruel pig-sticking fist with its thick fingers so lightly on my cheek.

I couldn't help it. I took his hand to my mouth and held it against my lips and kissed it. Pig blood and all. I kissed his hand again and again, with all its stink and fatty slime of dead pork. So he'd understand that I'd forgive him even if he killed me.

I was still holding his hand as he straighted up tall against the gray winter sky. He looked down at me and then he looked away. With his free arm he raked the sleeve of his work shirt across his eyes. It was the first time I ever seen him do it.

The only time.

Chapter

15

Papa lived through the winter. He died in his sleep out in the barn on the third of May.

He was always up before I was. And when I went out to the barn that morning, all was still. He was lying on the straw bed that he rigged for himself, and I knew before I got to him that he was dead.

"Papa." I said his name just once. "It's all right. You can sleep this morning. No cause to rouse yourself. I'll do the chores. There's no need to work any more. You just rest."

I fed and watered Solomon and Daisy. And milked her. Then I threw some grain to the hens, made sure they had water, and collected the eggs. One was still wet from laying. I remember there was only seven eggs; five whites and two brown. I wiped off the specks and carried them up the hill to the cellar. Then I went into the kitchen where Mama and Aunt Carrie were already moving about. Now that I was thirteen I was taller than both of them. I put an arm around each one of them, and held them close to me.

"Put my meal in a basket," I said. "I'm taking Solomon into town to see Mr. Wilcox. Papa won't be coming up for breakfast. Not this morning, and not ever again. I'll be back in about two hours, but first I'll stop and tell Matty and Hume. And some others."

"You go," Mama said. "Carrie and I will make do just fine. There's not time to tell your sisters. And scattered all over Vermont, they couldn't come."

"I'll write letters to all four," I said. "Now about the funeral. Does he have any good clothes?"

"Yes," Mama said. "They been ready for some time, up in the camphor chest at the foot of . . . our bed."

"Mama, if you could get them out and be ready when Mr. Wilcox comes, it would be a help."

"They'll be," she said.

I kissed each one of them on the brow, and went outside to yoke up the ox. I stopped Solomon at the front gate, went inside and got something (which I never did eat) tied up in a clean checkered napkin and went into Learning.

I told Mr. Wilcox, who was a good Shaker man and who took care of our dead. After telling Aunt Matty and Hume, I came on home. I made just two more stops. To tell Mrs. Bascom and Ira, and to tell Mr. and Mrs. Tanner. By the time I got home, Mr. Wilcox was already there. His bay gelding was just outside the barn hitched to a small rig. Behind the driver's bench was a coffin. It was unpainted wood and there were no handles. It was a gift from the Circle of Shakers in the town of Learning. Somewhere I'd find money to pay Mr. Wilcox. His fee would not be high as he was also the County Coroner.

"People will be coming at noon, Mr. Wilcox," I said to him, as he was preparing Papa.

"Everything will be ready, Robert."

"Thank you, sir."

I told Aunt Carrie and Mama about the time of the funeral. I knew they'd be ready, in their best and plainest.

"They won't be many coming," I said. "Maybe six and that's all."

"Rob," Mama said, "I'm glad we've got you to handle things. I couldn't of done it alone."

"Yes, you could, Mama. When you're the only one to do something, it always gets done."

I dug a grave in the family plot in our orchard.

After that I hunted for a chore, just anything to do. The day before Papa died, we'd been mending a plowshare out in the tackroom. Instead of just waiting for the people to come, I worked on it a bit. And just about got it righted.

Before I walked out of the tackroom, I noticed something I'd not took note of previous. It was the handles of Papa's tools. Most of the tools were dark with age, and their handles were a deep brown. But where Papa's hands had took a purchase on them, they were lighter in color. Almost a gold. The wear of his labor had made them smooth and shiny, where his fingers had held each one. I looked at all the handles of his tools. It was real beautiful the way they was gilded by work.

As I stood there looking over his tools, I had the hanker to reach out and touch them all. To hold them in my hands the same way he did, just to see if my hands were sized enough to take hold.

Under the tools, I saw an old cigar box that was gray with dust. Inside was a wore-down pencil stub and a scrap of old paper. Unfolding the paper, I saw where Papa had been trying to write his name. One of the "Haven Pecks" was near to perfect, and he almost had the hang of it. The paper was dry and brown, as if he had practiced for a long time. Carefully folding the paper back into just the way he had folded it, I rested it in its box and closed the lid.

Then I went inside to change clothes, as it was almost noon. As a young boy, I'd had a black suit that Mama made me. But I always felt like a preacher in it. Besides, now it was way too small. And what Papa owned was too spare. So I just put on a new pair of work shoes that were tan, and a pair of Papa's old black trousers which I turned up inside and stuck with pins. I wore one of his shirts with no necktie. I looked at myself in the mirror, to make sure I had the dignity to lead a family to a grave. I looked more like a clown than a mourner. The shirt didn't fit at all. And the tan work shoes just stuck out like I was almost barefoot. I ripped the shirt off and threw it on the floor. "Hear me, God," I said. "It's hell to be poor."

By noon, they'd all come. Just after we got Papa dressed and his coffin into the house.

Aunt Matty and Hume were the first. Mrs. Bascom came with Ira Long. Only her name was now Mrs. Long, legal and proper. But in my mind she always was Mrs. Bascom. Mr. Tanner and his wife came in the black rig, with a pair of black horses. I went out to meet them.

"Thank you for coming, Mr. Tanner."

"Robert, my name is Benjamin Franklin Tanner. All my neighbors call me Ben. I think two men who are good friends ought to front name one another."

"And I'm Bess," his wife said, "from here on."

As the Tanners joined the others in the parlor of the house, I looked up road. Another wagon was coming. It was May and Sebring Hillman. And from town came Isadore Crookshank along with Jacob Henry and his folks. Last to come was Mr. Clay Sander, the man my father slaughtered for. Along with several of the men that Papa worked with. There would be no work on this day. A day no pigs would die.

I was glad they came. Some of them were dressed no better than I. And some not even as well, but they came. They came to help us plant Haven Peck into the earth, and that was all that counted. They'd come because they respected him and honored him. As I looked at all them, standing uneasy in our small parlor, I was happy for Papa. He wasn't rich. But by damn he wasn't poor. He always said he wasn't poor, but I figured he was just having fun with himself. But he was sober. He had a lot, Papa did.

The coffin was open and lying on the long table in the kitchen. It was the only place for it to be under our roof. Papa was a tall man. But he was not to be seen from the parlor where all our friends gathered, and I was just as pleased. A man can't rest when he's looked at.

As eldest son, it was my place to say words about my father. I didn't know what I was going to say. It wouldn't be much. What I thought about Papa couldn't of been said. Being his son was like knowing a king. "Haven Peck," I said. "Devoted husband and father, a working farmer and a good neighbor. Beloved by wife, four daughters, and one living son. We are all grateful to know him. And we ask only that his soul enter the Kingdom Hall, there to abide forever."

Mr. Wilcox had coached me a bit as to proper words, so I guess I did all right. We left the parlor and filed through the kitchen, to look at Papa for one last time. Lots of folks said "Amen" as they passed by.

We closed the box of raw unpainted wood, nailing down the lid. Then six of the men raised it up, and walked with it out to the grave I dug in the orchard. With lowering ropes, they let it down into the ground onto two small cross boards, so that they could pull the two ropes out again. There was something in the Book of Shaker that it was unfit to bury the ropes with a coffin. Probably because rope was so dearly priced. It would be an earthy reason.

I had placed two shovels there at the open grave.

As soon as the coffin was down, Ira Long and Se-bring Hillman (two of the sturdiest) started to shovel the soil into the hole. The first shovelfuls had some Vermont rock in them, and the stones hit the wood like a drum. But then as more and more dirt was added, it sounded softer and softer. When all the earth was finally replaced, they packed it down with the flat of their spades. There was no marker, no headstone. Nothing to say who it was or what he had done in his sixty years.

We all walked away then, Aunt Carrie and Mama on either side of me. They both looked and walked so proper, and I was proud to be between them. Mama's sweet face was so plain and so empty. What she missed most was not to be spoken of. We all would long for a different parcel of him.

"Rob," said Ben Tanner, as everyone took leave, "if Bess or me can lend a hand or help in any way, just ask."

"Thank you, Ben," I said. "You're a goodly neigh-bor."

"The way you said that," Ben said, "you sort of sounded like your father."

"I aim to, Ben."

Then they were gone. Mama and Aunt Carrie were busy in the house, scolding each other to keep from weeping. I changed into my work clothes, and scraped a wood shim for the door of the milk house.

Solomon had a cut on his eye (I didn't know from what) and I treated it with boric best I could. I cleaned up the tackroom and sharpened a scythe. I cut a fresh sassafras tree and prepared it so as it could boil into a new bow for Solomon's yoke, and bored a hole in both ends for the cotter pins.

At chore time, I pailed Daisy. Fed, watered, cleaned, and put down fresh straw. Then I ate supper with Aunt Carrie and Mama. There wasn't much to eat, except beans. And we'd lived on those all winter. Beans and pork. And none of it was easy to swallow.

After the supper dishes were washed and dry, I could see how tired Mama looked. Carrie, too. So I sent them upstairs to bed, each with a hot cup of tea.

As I knew I couldn't sleep, I put on my coat and walked outside. I took a look in on Daisy and Solomon, and they were both quiet as vespers. Both of them were getting old, and they liked being in the barn. Even on a nice spring night such as this.

Something brushed against my ankle. It was Miss Sarah, just to say hello. Before she went out on the meadow to hunt moles.

I don't know why I walked out toward the orchard. All the work there was done. But I guess I had to give a goodnight to Papa, and be alone with him. The bugs were out, and their singing was all around me. Almost like a choir. I got to the fresh grave, all neatly mounded and pounded. Somewhere down under all that Vermont clay was my father, Haven Peck. Buried deep in the land he sweated so hard on and longed to own so much. And now it owned him.

"Goodnight, Papa," I said. "We had thirteen good years."

That was all I could say, so I just turned and walked away from a patch of grassless land.

About the Author

Raised in the Shaker tradition, like many Vermont folk, the author was taught as a boy to live and work in the Shaker Way that endured even after the sect itself had died out. Its earthy reason is embodied in Haven Peck who believed that a faith is more blessed when put to use than when put to word: "A man's worship counts for naught, unless his dog and cat are better for it."

A Note on the Type

This book was set in Granjon, a type named in compliment to Robert Granjon, type cutter and printer—in Antwerp, Lyons, Rome, Paris—active from 1523 to 1590. The boldest and most original designer of his time, he was one of the first to practice the trade of type founder apart from that of printer.

This type face was designed by George W. Jones, who based his drawings on a type used by Claude Garamond (1510–61) in his beautiful French books, and it more closely resembles Garamond's own type than do any of the various modern types that bear his name.

E